Atlatl Press
POB 521
Dayton, Ohio 45401
atlatlpress.com
info@atlatlpress.com

Murder House
Copyright © 2020 by C.V. Hunt
Cover design copyright © 2020 by Squidbar Designs
Paperback ISBN-13: 978-1-941918-67-8

This book is a work of fiction. Names, characters, business organizations, places, events, and incidents either are the product of the author's imagination or are used fictitiously. The author's use of names of actual persons (living or dead), places, and characters is incidental to the purposes of the plot, and is not intended to change the entirely fictional character of the work.

No part of this work may be reproduced, stored in a retrieval system, or transmitted by any means without the written permission of the author or publisher.

Other titles by C.V. Hunt

How To Kill Yourself
Zombieville
Thanks For Ruining My Life
Other People's Shit
Baby Hater
Hell's Waiting Room
Misery and Death and Everything Depressing
Ritualistic Human Sacrifice
Poor Decisions
We Did Everything Wrong
Home Is Where the Horror Is
Hold For Release Until the End of the World
Cockblock
Halloween Fiend

For Andy

I'm glad we get to spend the apocalypse together.

**Source: The Detroit Free Press, November 1, 1975
Headline: Hallows' Eve Massacre!**

On Friday, October 31, police were dispatched to the Delany neighborhood near the Detroit River. Neighbors called the police to complain about loud banging and screaming coming from a residence on Crossley Street. Concerned residents told police they did not believe the noise was part of the Halloween festivities. Police arrived on the scene shortly after 10 PM and found James Dobos (40) sitting on the front steps of 732 South Crossley Street. Dobos appeared dazed and in shock. When police approached Mr. Dobos he refused to answer any direct questions and officers noticed blood on his hands and clothing.

"He (James Dobos) kept rocking back and forth and mumbling *they* were trying to poison him. He was yammering something about his family had made a deal with the devil and they were going to sacrifice him and the children and the devil was coming in the house at night from the basement," Sheriff Michael Lawson of the Detroit

Police Department, Southwest District said. "I'd never seen such a sight. We weren't prepared for what we discovered inside."

Officers entered the home on Crossley Street to find ten of James Dobos' family members deceased and scattered throughout the house. All the victims had suffered from what appeared to be various and numerous knife wounds. Some of the family members had been eviscerated and some were missing their extremities. There also appeared to be several bite wounds on the deceased. No murder weapon was found amongst the dead nor were the severed limbs recovered. Of the deceased were James Dobos' mother, Hope Dobos (65), his brother, Leon Dobos (42), his sister-in-law, Ana Dobos (41), and Leon and Ana's seven children: Leon Jr. (16), Timothy (14), Anne (12), Theresa (11), Daniel (9), John (5), Carol (2).

"It was terrible. So terrible," Deputy Joseph McCoy said. "The children were in their costumes. There was gore and candy everywhere. The two youngest were in the basement. There was so much blood it was dripping between the floorboards of the first floor and pooling in the basement. I hope I never have to see something like that ever again."

Police aren't sure what prompted Dobos to slay his entire family but several of the neighbors told police James was a taciturn man who was either unable or unwilling to work. He resided in the home with his mother. Hope and Leon Dobos contributed walking-around money to James, which neighbors said he spent nightly at Kovacs Bar.

"He'd get to drinking and he'd tell wild tales," frequent customer of Kovacs Bar, David Hornok, said when questioned by our reporters. Hornok added, "Always talking about how he was being poisoned and his head didn't feel right. Said his brother was going to murder him one day and feed him to the devil." David Hornok shrugged before stating, "I thought it was drunk talk."

Fellow neighbor, Janice Kemeny, attended Holy Cross Hungarian Church with Hope Dobos. She said, "Hope was fed up with James.

The only time he left the house was to go to the bar and spend the money she'd given him. He was a strange fellow. Always talking to himself about the devil but he wouldn't go to church. I'm glad I don't let my children participate in all the Halloween shenanigans. Puts the devil in their heads and god-fearing children don't need any of that."

The slaying of the Dobos family members turned Beggar's Night into something more horrifying than anyone could imagine. Funeral arrangements for the deceased family members are being planned. We will provide updates on this story as police disclose more information.

ONE

WE PASSED ONE empty and overgrown lot after another. The area reminded me of something from an apocalyptic movie I vaguely remember watching as a child. I tried to recall the name of the flick but kept drawing a blank. The vibe of the area felt wrong. The neighborhood felt off in a large city like Detroit. I'd heard stories and seen pictures of urban decay but couldn't quite wrap my head around it until we began to drive through it. Most of the lots were devoid of buildings and had at least waist-high weeds. If there was a house, the windows and doors had been hastily boarded up. But more often than not, the lot held a partially collapsed house with no effort put into securing the broken windows or the missing or kicked-in doors. What few houses we'd seen in the last five minutes appeared to be in such a state I didn't think even squatters would take up residence in them.

Roofs were collapsed. Windows were gone. Doors were ajar. One faded blue house had 'THERE IN THE SEWER' spray-painted across the front of the house.

I half expected Brent to say something about the typo but he kept his eyes on the road, wearing a determined expression, one that made him look angry to anyone who didn't know him well. It was a look I'd grown accustomed to over the years. The furrowed brow. The pursed lips. It was the same face he made when writing. As if the words or the laptop screen had done something to offend him somehow.

Brent drove over a sizable pothole and our belongings rattled in the back of the station wagon. I noticed his eyes flicking up to the rearview mirror and back to the road. I knew he didn't care much for the few items we'd brought with us but if anything happened to his laptop or printer I knew the world might as well end for him. I recalled the time the motherboard crapped out on his previous laptop and the near hysterical meltdown I endured for a week while he shopped for a new one and toted the useless one from repair shop to repair shop, trying desperately to retrieve thirty-five thousand words of the book he was working on. That was the time I learned not to offer any encouraging sentiments such as 'maybe it happened for a reason and the next draft will be even better' unless I wanted him to offer up such biting remarks as 'you don't understand because you're not a writer' and 'maybe if you were passionate about something other than sitting on the sofa and watching television you'd comprehend the situation.' It got ugly. That was two years ago and the only time I seriously considered packing my things and leaving, although the list of offenses previous and since would be more than enough for most people to be gone in a flash. The admiration of finding a guy with a brain and an artistic passion nearly a decade earlier died after his remarks. Our relationship hadn't been the same since but neither of us brought it up or talked about it. And honestly, I wasn't really sure whether Brent was even aware there was a problem. In the two years since, he'd grown cold and distant and acted as if my mere existence and the fact I was breathing aggravated him. I chalked it up to the quirks of an artist, and the stress of our financial situation would test even the strongest relationship.

"Laura," Brent said harshly.

I was pulled back from my retrospection and turned to him. "Hmm?"

He sighed and there was an air of irritation in his tone. "You should probably start researching local thrift stores or scratch and dent shops if you want a bed to sleep in tonight."

The air of condescension in his tone stung but it wasn't anything I hadn't grown numb and accustomed to. I lifted my sore butt from the seat and retrieved my cell phone. After so many hours on the road I was looking forward to getting out of the car and standing. A bed was the least of my concerns. I thumbed the screen and pulled up a business review app and searched for used furniture stores. A used bed wasn't ideal but when you combined the income of a writer and a now-unemployed food server, funds were going to be scarce even with Brent's promised meager advance once the completed novel was submitted. We were fortunate enough the publisher was willing to shell out the cost of renting the house for us. They were desperate to jump on the true crime boom and hopeful enough to think they'd be able to recoup their costs once the book was hurriedly written and published. They'd given Brent three months to write the thing and three months free rent in the murder house. It was muggy and hot now at the beginning of August. Who knew what the weather would be like at the end of October. By the looks of the houses we'd passed I didn't have much hope for the actual murder house and was certain it would be a drafty, spider-infested mess. The thought of staying much longer than October wasn't something I was looking forward to and didn't think Brent's publisher would budget a day over.

I'd found a couple of thrift stores that didn't look like they were crawling with bed bugs when the GPS announced our turn. Brent turned onto a side road. I looked up to see a brick building housing a mom and pop hardware store and the local fire department facing the road we'd turned from. The road we were on was partially constructed from red brick and broken concrete. The first block on the street had an empty grass lot on the left and a huge cluster of overgrown trees and weeds on the right. It wasn't until we passed the trees that I spotted the glint of a window buried in the brush.

"There's a house in there," I said.

Brent didn't respond. He either hadn't heard me or didn't care. I was certain it was the latter.

The GPS announced our destination as we reached the next block. The right side of the road was another empty lot. But the left held a dilapidated house with no trees or shrubs in the yard. Brent pulled into the driveway and I took in our new temporary home.

It was a dirty tan house with a worn and nearly crumbling brown roof. The rickety front porch was missing a door. What windows weren't boarded up looked filthy and the whole structure appeared to have been steeped in water. It had a bloated appearance, as if there had been a flood at one point or another or rainwater had been left to seep in through the roof.

We exited the car. Brent immediately pulled the paper from his pocket with the numerical code to open the lockbox on the doorknob to retrieve the key. He approached the house as I took in the surroundings.

The mailbox was canted at an angle so severe I wasn't sure it was okay to use or not. The next block was the last as the road came to a dead end but it was still home to what appeared to be an abandoned church. Since there weren't any other houses on our block I could spot a row of five houses the next road over. Three of them definitely looked abandoned but the one nestled in the middle had an old car parked in the drive. Even though the car looked decrepit I was sure it ran as all four tires were inflated. I couldn't say the same for the car parked in front of the last house, its windows shattered and the tires completely missing. I guess the police or whoever kept an eye on the area weren't concerned with its violation.

Banging came from the porch. I opened the back door of the car and retrieved a box of cleaning supplies and approached the open doorway and watched as Brent held the doorknob and slammed his shoulder into the swollen wooden door. I thought about warning him to not dislocate his shoulder or destroy the door but thought better of it. I knew it would only start an argument or rouse him to give me that silent disgusted look I despised and sometimes made me want to slap him. The door finally broke free and opened into the darkness of the house.

TWO

THE INSIDE OF the house looked as bad as the outside. Maybe worse. I was surprised the lights actually worked. The bulbs were filthy and cast a sickly yellow hue over everything. Brent had switched them on before disappearing to wherever. I took a deep breath and tried not to be pissed because I knew he wasn't going to help me unload the car. Resignation had been my life motto for a long time now. I knew he'd be too interested in exploring the house and I'd be the one lugging most of our stuff in. I'd only taken a few steps into the living area, holding the box, and nearly fell. The floors were warped and swollen. They didn't look like anything you could walk across without shoes unless you wanted to dig splinters out of your feet. I'd caught the toe of my shoe on one of the misshapen boards.

The walls of the parlor and living area were covered in a garish forest green wallpaper with gaudy mauve flowers that appeared to be made of cloth. There was a set of sliding French doors to another room on the left with intricate carvings in the woodwork frame. I looked to the left and spotted the kitchen and headed toward it as Brent appeared from the basement door located between the kitchen and living area.

"There's no lights in the basement," he said.

"We'll pick up some bulbs while we're out."

"There's not even a light socket down there for a light. We'll need to get a flashlight or lantern or something."

I set the box on the dirty kitchen counter. "A lantern? Where do you get a lantern?"

His eyelids fluttered and I was certain he was fighting the urge to roll his eyes at my ignorance. Without a word he tromped off to another part of the house.

The kitchen counter was covered with Formica laminate and someone had poorly nailed silver trim around the edges. It was evident the trim had been caught on something and bent and nailed back down. The kinks looked sharp, like they were aching for blood. I tried to remember the last time I had a tetanus shot. The cabinets were outdated and a few of the doors were missing. I opened one of the drawers and spotted mouse droppings. I checked the refrigerator. It smelled like death and rotten food and appeared as if it hadn't been cleaned in a decade. I retrieved a bottle of bleach cleaner and a roll of paper towels from the box and made quick work of cleaning the counter, drawers, cabinets, and refrigerator, throwing the spent paper towels in the sink until there was a sizable amount before retrieving the box of trash bags.

The entire time I was hurriedly cleaning the kitchen Brent was stomping through the house, exploring every nook and cranny. I kept thinking at some point he would begin unpacking the car. I don't know why I thought he would actually help. We'd been together for fifteen years. I knew better. I was surprised he hadn't begun hassling me to start unloading the car already, as it would need to be unloaded before we could find a bed.

I turned on the water in the sink to wash my hands before attempting to pull the phone from my back pocket. I didn't want to get bleach stains on my jeans. The pipes groaned and rusty brown water spat from the faucet, hit the porcelain sink, and splashed up on my shirt. I cussed and stepped back as the water farted into the sink and finally ran clear. Luckily my shirt was black so whatever was in the water, probably rust, wouldn't stain it. When everything you owned came from a thrift store and you didn't have money to replace anything should it break or fail, you were careful to baby everything, regardless of how worn or dilapidated it was. And dark-colored clothing was the best option when living on a budget. You didn't need hot water or bleach to do laundry if everything you owned was dark.

I let the water run over my hands, continually fiddling with the nozzle, trying to produce something remotely resembling warm water. The hot water alone had terrible water pressure and took forever to warm. I was certain my stream of urine had more pressure. I was starting to wonder if the hot water heater was broken or if the pilot light needed lighting when it finally began to feel lukewarm.

I cleaned my hands and checked the time on my phone. We had six more hours before the nearest used furniture store closed. I really wanted to clean the bathroom and do a quick sweep and dust of the bedroom before we did anything else.

I didn't think the layer of filth could get much worse until I checked out the bathroom. The toilet was more than disgusting and someone had decided that painting the shower walls was easier than cleaning the thick layer of soap scum. Paint was flaking off the shower wall and littering the tub floor. Some genius thought putting down carpet in the bathroom was a good idea, probably to keep from getting splinters if the floor underneath was like the rest of the house. The penetrating smell of mold and mildew from the carpeted floor stung my eyes and made my chest tight. I would've opened the window but, being on the first floor, the property owner had nailed a piece of plywood over it on the outside.

It was going to take way too long to clean the bathroom and I knew we were going to have to remove the carpet if neither of us wanted to end up in the hospital with some sort of rare lung disease. I dumped some bleach in the toilet and cleaned it and the vanity.

When I'd done what I could with the bathroom I went to find Brent. I climbed the stairs to the second floor and found him in the upstairs hallway. His back was to me. He had his hands on his hips and was staring at a pull cord for the attic door in the ceiling.

I stopped behind him. "I think we need to pull the—"

He flinched and spun to face me. "Jesus! Could you not sneak up on me like that?"

"Sorry. Would've thought you could hear me climbing the creaky ass steps." I pointed to the stairs behind me. "The carpet in the bathroom needs to go. It's all moldy. Do you think the landlord would mind?"

He frowned and turned back to look at the ceiling. I wanted to repeat that we needed to pull the carpet from the bathroom but I knew it was pointless, as he'd either ignore me or brush it off until I did it myself. So I decided to go with what I knew he'd be more concerned with.

"We need to unpack the car so we can get a bed."

He sighed and muttered something I didn't catch. I was certain it was a snarky remark asking why I hadn't already unloaded the car myself. Getting him to do anything today would be impossible and repeatedly asking him to help would end badly, with him accusing me of nagging him. I left him in the hallway and took it upon myself to unload everything into the kitchen since that's where the majority of it would be anyway. I was sweaty and exhausted when I was done but knew I had to keep moving because the moment I sat down was the moment I would feel every muscle in my body protesting.

My thighs ached as I climbed the stairs to find Brent again. The attic ladder had been let down and I could make out a light shuffling sound coming from the opening in the ceiling.

As I approached the wooden ladder I thought I heard someone whispering. I stepped on the first rung and the whole contraption felt as if it might break away from the ceiling. It made me feel uneasy and even though there wasn't much distance from the floor to the attic I had a terrible fear of heights, even five or six feet up on a ladder would make my stomach hurt and cause my palms to sweat. I thought better of ascending any farther.

"Brent," I called up into the dark opening in the ceiling.

No answer. For some reason this raised the hair on the back of my neck.

Out of fear I called out sharply, "Brent!"

From behind me came an aggravated answer. "What?"

I started. I gripped the precarious rails of the ladder and the wood groaned in protest. The first fold of the ladder began to buckle in the opposite direction. But stopped abruptly.

"Jesus, Laura, don't break the fucking ladder!"

I regained my balance and stepped down. My heart was racing when I spun to Brent. "I thought you were in the attic. I heard you shuffling through things up there."

"I was in the bedroom." He paused and assessed me as if he couldn't believe I could be so stupid. "You probably heard mice fucking around up there."

"I guess we should add mice traps to the list," I said. "The car is unpacked. We should get going before the stores close."

He nodded and headed toward the stairs for the first floor. I turned back to the attic ladder and swore I heard someone whispering again.

THREE

NOTHING MAKES YOU feel poor and unwanted like haggling over the price of a used mattress. I hated it. I spent most of my time distancing myself from Brent as he tried to get the manager—a heavyset man with greasy hair and an equally greasy face—to drop the price fifty dollars. Fifty dollars for most people wasn't a big deal but our funds were extremely limited. I could only hope to find a job by the end of the month or I wasn't sure what we were going to do. Maybe Brent could ask for an advance on his advance. Was that even possible?

The publisher was taking care of the basic utilities and the house but that didn't cover food or the prepaid cell phone. We'd bit the bullet and paid for one more month of data and talk time to navigate here and have a source of contact for research. Brent had previously decided to take his laptop to the library if he needed. He hadn't asked about an internet connection and didn't want to assume they'd provide one so he was prepared to leave the house occasionally and go to whatever coffee shop that would let him hang around all day without buying anything if he had to.

I pretended to look at some ugly drapes I was certain were at least fifty years old while Brent switched tactics and went for the old heartstrings. The manager looked like those had been broken by life several decades ago. I knew that dead inside blank stare anywhere. I wasn't sure about anyone else who struggled with the same affliction but I knew my own ilk when I saw them.

Brent spoke in a gentle and pleading tone so unlike him I had to double-check and make sure it was still him talking to the greasy manager. "I know it's asking a lot but we just moved here and my wife is pregnant." He gestured in my direction.

The manager turned his cow-like gaze on me. I tried to smile but I'd never been a good bullshitter. I hated to lie.

The words 'wife' and 'pregnant' were laughable. I sure as fuck wouldn't marry Brent if he begged me and my chances of having a kid went with my uterus after a horrendous case of endometriosis in my twenties before I met Brent. The thought of marriage made me feel more trapped than I already was and made my chest feel tight whenever I even briefly considered it. The thought of signing a binding contract attaching myself to another human being that would be impossible to sever due to a lack of financial means wasn't something I had ever pondered. And I would need a lot of money to leave Brent since I didn't have any friends or family to really speak of. Friends consisted of coworkers who didn't get on my nerves and make me feel like shit. But I wasn't really sure I could consider them friends as there wasn't any tears shed between myself or them when I told them on short notice I was quitting and we were relocating, unsure if we'd ever return.

Brent addressed the manager, "Please don't make me tell her she has to sleep on the floor tonight."

The manager never took his eyes from me and spoke in a monotone. "She don't look pregnant."

I slipped behind the rack of drapes and heard Brent tell him I was only twelve weeks along before the manager agreed to drop the price. Brent also managed to get the guy to call on a couple of the employees to tie the mattress to the roof of the car. I thought this was more out of Brent's insatiable ability to wiggle out of doing anything physical than to keep up the ruse that I was pregnant. We knew we'd pushed our luck at that point and moved on to the next store and managed to get a pretty beat-up breakfast table and chair set for two.

By the time we'd secured a bed and some place to sit and eat, it was growing late. I searched on the cell and found a Dollar General nearby. When we pulled into the lot I spotted a man in dirty clothing digging through the dumpster peeking out from behind the building. He had the handle of a baby stroller tied to the back of a rusted Huffy bicycle. The stroller was loaded with various pieces of metal. Someone had spray painted 'It will make you difrent' on the brick exterior of the store. I expected Brent to say something about this typo this time but he seemed too preoccupied as we hurried into the store.

The aisles were crammed with unopened and spilled boxes of merchandise the hard and worn looking employees had chosen to dump there instead of placing the items on the shelves. It made it difficult to find anything. We finally found a flashlight, batteries, and some wooden mouse traps. I made sure to get a couple of cans of disinfectant spray and some food. Although we had a mattress it had some questionable stains. I'd checked it thoroughly for any signs of bedbugs but knew everything purchased secondhand was a crapshoot. Used clothes you could throw in the wash. With furniture, you were kind of fucked.

Brent was quiet on the way home. The car windows were down and I welcomed the breeze. I was sweaty and exhausted and watched the fireflies rising up and blinking. The locusts and katydids were in full swing and filled the evening air with their screams. I was too tired to carry on a conversation even if I wanted to.

When we got home it took the last bit of energy to drag the mattress in the house. We decided the living room was good enough for the moment. I sprayed the mattress with disinfectant and put the sheets on it. We both chugged water from the tap, which tasted off, before I returned to the mattress and collapsed on it. I vaguely recalled Brent plugging in a box fan and scavenging through the store bags for a granola bar. I remembered thinking I should get up and get something to eat and shower but I was asleep before I could complete the thought.

FOUR

I WOKE IN the middle of the night from a horrible nightmare. I was sweating and tried desperately to grasp at whatever terrible thing that happened in the dream but the only thing I could recollect upon waking was that there was something invading my body, controlling my every move no matter how hard I fought it.

The light above the kitchen sink was on and cast a strangled light into the living area. My heart leapt again as I spotted the faint outline of a naked man standing in front of the open basement door. I reached beside me to wake Brent as the surge of fear and adrenaline cleared the sleep from my brain and I realized as I touched the cool empty mattress beside me it was Brent standing nude, staring down into the darkened void of the basement. I could smell the dank and dusty concrete of the basement and thought I could detect a slight, cool breeze pulsing from the depths as if it were a living and breathing

thing.

"Brent," I croaked. My vocal cords were heavy with sleep.

Brent didn't move or make any acknowledgment he'd heard me.

"What are you doing?" I said.

No response. The hairs on the back of my neck came to attention. I rose from the mattress and approached him. Once I reached him, I simultaneously said his name and touched his shoulder. He sucked in a deep breath as if emerging from water and spun toward me. His eyes were open wide and the light from the kitchen made them appear glassy. He looked crazed.

"What are you doing?" he barked. He looked around wildly as if he wasn't aware of where he was. "What's going on?" He looked down and, I believe, realized for the first time he was naked.

His confusion confused me. "I don't know," I said. "I think you're sleep walking?"

He blinked rapidly. "Then you're not supposed to wake me."

"Sorry. I was worried about you. You didn't answer me. It was creepy and freaked me out."

He'd lost interest in anything I was saying and looked beyond me. He stepped around me and retrieved something from the floor. He bent and lifted his leg. I realized the something on the floor was a pile of clothing. He quickly pulled on his underwear.

I found the phone by my pillow and checked the time. It was four in the morning and the battery on the phone was nearly dead. Brent went to the bathroom to relieve himself and I dug around in one of the boxes and retrieved the phone's charging cord and plugged it in by the kitchen sink.

I stripped down to my underwear. I'd fallen asleep fully clothed and the sweat had made my clothes damp.

Brent returned to the mattress and lay down, facing away from me.

"That was weird," I said. I wanted him to at least talk to me for a minute to calm my nerves but he only grunted in return.

As much as I tried, I couldn't fall back asleep. Every faint noise the house produced sounded ominous and alive. It was only a few moments before Brent's snores drowned it all out and I spent the rest of the night staring at the open basement door and the darkness beyond. I was too frightened to get up and close it.

FIVE

AFTER BREAKFAST BRENT took up residence at the kitchen table and began writing. My day was going to be filled with the clicking of his keyboard and his frustrated sighs as he worked. I was glad I'd tackled the kitchen counters previously and all that was left to do in there was the floor. I'd wait until he moved before attempting it if I didn't want to be the target of pointed sighs and half-muttered curses.

My first task was to find the hammer and screwdriver, the only two tools we owned, and remove the plywood covering the first-floor windows so they could be opened. Once that was done I covered my face with a shirt and dug into the bathroom carpet. Nothing could be done to keep my eyes from burning as I worked. Landlord be damned, the carpet was a safety hazard.

Removing the carpet revealed a dark stain on the moldy wood

beneath. I scrubbed for what felt like hours and even though the mold—which was most likely toxic or deadly—came up easily enough, the dark stain didn't budge.

Brent appeared in the bathroom doorway and stared at the floor as I scrubbed.

I pulled the shirt off my nose and mouth and said, "The floor is stained to hell but I think I got the mold."

"That's probably a blood stain," he said.

I made a disgusted sound and tossed the scrub brush in the bucket as if the brush itself was a turd. I tried to jump up quickly. The thought of a dead body lying in the exact spot gave me the creeps, but forty years hadn't been kind to my joints. I gripped the sink and pulled myself up.

"Gross," I said. I made more disgusted sounds.

Brent's eyelids twitched. He fought an eyeroll. "We're staying in a murder house. The whole thing is saturated in death. You might want to get used to it."

"I didn't think anyone was killed in the bathroom."

"Carol Dobos."

He paused as if he was allowing me to realize who he was referring to but I didn't and I hadn't read up on any of the murders. The less I knew, the better I felt about the situation. Ignorance was bliss.

He said, "Can I get in here? I need to defecate."

I stepped out of the bathroom and made my way to the kitchen. I flopped down on a kitchen chair and retrieved the phone from my pocket and searched 'Carol Dobos murder Detroit.' Nothing came up immediately so I clicked on images.

The first photo was a grainy black and white photo someone had poorly positioned on a scanner and uploaded. In the photo a toddler lay on the floor of our bathroom. The sink was the same but the tub was an old claw foot tub. Someone had changed the tub at one point or another. The toddler was wearing an oversized plastic Halloween smock and one of those old plastic masks with the stapled elastic bands to hold it in place. I wasn't able to tell exactly what the costume was as the smock was ripped, her internal organs scattered on the floor, and she was covered in a dark substance I knew was blood.

Without warning, my stomach began to churn and I bolted to the sink and managed to make it in time to lose the contents of my stomach. This was why the less I knew about the murders the better.

SIX

SOMETHING SHIFTS IN your mind after certain life events. It's almost a physical thing. The movement of a fetus as it swims in its mother's womb. You can never be sure if it's something good or bad. If it's the twitch of something new growing and about to be born or the death throes of a former you. A light switch. There one second and gone the next, never to be regained. Like losing your virginity. An insight into something new or possibly a curse. A pane of glass cracking. It can never be repaired, only replaced.

It's something that happens. You can't stop it. And it happens in a split second. You can try to explain it to the people around you but unless you've been through it yourself you can never really grasp the finality of it. For most people it comes after a realization. It hits you one morning when you wake up, step into the bathroom, and take a good long look at yourself. This usually happens in your early thirties.

You gaze into the mirror and you realize you've gotten old. You see the beginnings of the fine lines which will deepen and spread as each day passes. There's no turning back unless you have the time and money to dump into a plastic surgery addiction. In which case you'll end up looking like an even bigger monster. One that has been scrubbed of any detail or true identity. Something smooth as a newborn but unnatural since you're more than halfway into the grave and full of silicone.

You see those awful and offending lines reflected in the mirror. The ones screaming your youth is dead. You're old and getting older and you haven't done a damn thing with your life. They're the same lines you watched crawl across your father's face when you were a teen and thought, *God, I hope I never get old*. Or you start to see the reformation of your jawline. The softening of the jowls. The sagging of the neck skin. The image in the mirror says, "Fuck. I'm turning into my mother/father," in sync with your own proclamation.

For others the break comes after the death of a parent. Or both parents. The graduation of a child. The birth of a grandchild. A divorce. Becoming a widow(er). Some people can tell you the exact minute they came face to face with their mortality. Others, it happens gradually.

Mine came when I realized I wasn't in love with Brent anymore. Or maybe it was when I realized he wasn't in love with me anymore. If he ever really had been in love with me. It felt like I was a convenience for him. Someone who tolerated his mood swings and paid the bills. I wasn't really sure if I was resentful because he'd taken the best years of my youth or because I'd essentially become his mother and a work horse. It didn't help that I couldn't talk to him about it. Every time I attempted to talk about my feelings he shut down and I could tell he didn't give a fuck. He was waiting for his turn to talk about what he wanted to talk about or for me to shut up so he could get back to his keyboard.

Eventually I shut down. I felt things in my brain slipping. Like a grain of sand in an hour glass. Inevitably, it would fall through the crack and be buried by the other thousands of pieces of sand and forgotten. Just a number. Just a cog in the machine. My thoughts grew increasingly foggy and my ability to remember things completely shit out. I became increasingly confused during conversations. So much that Brent grew angry with me and made me see a doctor, convinced I had early onset dementia. Turns out depression can really fuck with your head. Dysthymia is what the doctor called it. A low-grade persistent depression I'd been struggling with since puberty. But a person can also experience an onset of major depression superimposed on their dysthymic disorder and then you're diagnosed with what the doctor referred to as double depression. It all sounded like something completely made up to me but I took the medication as prescribed and I was pretty sure it had knocked the major depression some. But I knew something still wasn't right with my head. I could feel it. But I went through the motions every day. Took my meds. Put on a smile. And pretended everything was okay.

I didn't have anyone to talk to about it. My parents had died shortly after high school. My other siblings were disasters. I wasn't even sure if my oldest brother was still alive. And making friends was impossible when you were bullied all throughout school and never developed the social skills or drive to be surrounded by people. The doctor shoved prescriptions I was barely able to afford at me. I sure as hell didn't have the money for therapy. Therapy seemed like a thing only rich people paid for when they didn't have any friends or family members to talk to or they didn't have any friends or family who gave enough of a shit to listen to them whine about their problems.

Now I stood in the dank bathroom with the last pill of my prescription in my palm, wondering and slightly panicking about what was going to happen when the medicine was finally eliminated from my body. We didn't have the money for me to continue taking the medication. It wasn't like it was something I needed to take to stay alive or physically healthy. Thankfully I didn't have some grave heart condition or cancer. This was depression. We had to make some financial cuts. Maybe once the publisher paid Brent or I found a job, hopefully one with insurance this time, I'd go back on it. It was only three months until Brent was paid. What's the worst that could happen?

SEVEN

BRENT CONVINCED THE publisher to pay for high-speed internet. He argued I needed the car to find a job and he wouldn't have access to transportation to get to a library. He added some biting remarks about them providing him with the tools to complete the job they'd asked for on time and that did the trick. Obviously, he did want me to find a job but more than anything he didn't want to have to get dressed every day and go scouting for an internet connection. The more he got to sit at home shirtless and in shorts the happier he'd be. Even if I didn't want to work I would find a job. I couldn't tolerate him sighing and huffing any time I stepped into the kitchen for a drink of water or the glares and mumbles of being a distraction I received if I happened to be within view of his makeshift desk in the kitchen and I was doing anything other than sitting perfectly still. I really wanted to mention that he could help me move the mattress upstairs and he wouldn't have to see me but, honestly, fuck him. If he was too self-involved to help me for five minutes I was completely fine with making him miserable by just being in his line of sight.

After a couple of weeks he also started complaining of a constant low-grade headache. I wasn't sure if it was a passive aggressive way to tell me to fuck off and leave him alone or if he were actually suffering from constant headaches. Either way, he was testier than usual and eating entirely too much Tylenol.

It made me sad to think back to a time when we used sex for ailments like headaches instead of Tylenol, the latter he was going through like they were his savior. I wasn't going to offer up any pussy though. Nothing I did or said was ever the right thing anymore. I knew after a few days of no antidepressants they were leaving my system because the mere thought of him rejecting my sexual advances had me on the verge of tears and every nerve in my body felt raw and exposed, like a sensitive tooth to the cold. I could blame a bit of my weepiness on exhaustion too since I was the only person who'd put every waking second into scrubbing the house down as best as I could. But I knew the majority of my low emotions were a lack of serotonin.

Every bout of depression wasn't exactly the same. But it wasn't so different you couldn't eventually realize what was happening. The episodes weren't twins but sisters. I could feel this might end up being one of the crying kind. Tears at the drop of a hat. I hated that type because it usually came with random aches and pains as if I were getting arthritis. But at least it didn't usually come with a lack of drive to do anything because there was a lot to do. Those were the worst.

I sat on the mattress and tried to look for a job on the phone but found myself staring at the screen with my thumb hovering over it. I was lost in thought, or lack of thought, and nothing else. I had to force myself to concentrate and remind myself I was looking for a job. The first thing I needed was the zip code and the thought of looking it up made me tired. I wasn't even sure what our address was and sure as hell didn't want to interrupt Brent to ask. I knew I needed to get up and go look at our house's address on the house but had to fight the urge to lie down and take a nap. As much as I wanted to sleep, I was certain Brent would find some way to make noise and wake me up and somehow make me feel guilty for lying around and sleeping when I should've been looking for a job.

The humidity was high and felt like a wet blanket and no matter how high the fan ran there was no getting comfortable. The heaviness of the air was making me sleepy.

Brent suddenly stopped typing. He rose from the table abruptly and walked into the living room. "I need the phone."

I held it out to him without question. I really didn't want to look for a job at the moment anyway. He took it and briefly glanced at the job posting I was trying to read before heading back to the kitchen.

He grumbled, "I gotta make a couple of calls."

I flopped back on the mattress and stared at the stained ceiling. A cool breeze wafted form the basement door and I could hear Brent introducing himself to someone and talking about the book he was writing. I got up and walked over to the basement door. The breeze stopped. I couldn't make anything out beyond a few steps. I hadn't been to the basement yet and it seemed like there should be windows down there to let in sunlight. The basement creeped me out and there really was no need for me to go down there. But there had to be an opening if there was a breeze.

Brent had left the flashlight on the floor by the door. I picked it up and turned it on, half expecting Brent to say something but he was too preoccupied with whoever he was speaking with. I shone the light down the wooden stairs and could make out the crumbling red brick walls. I didn't have a desire to go down there. But there was nothing to do since Brent had the phone and we didn't own a television.

Another cool but faint gust of air that smelled of dirt and decay hit my sweaty skin and felt good. And for some reason I couldn't fathom I began to descend the rickety stairs. The temperature dropped and made my skin prick.

I panned the light around once I reached the bottom of the stairs. There were several handmade shelves painted a sickly mint green. The shelves housed rusted paint cans and a thick layer of cobwebs. A rusty tricycle sat in the corner and gave me the heebie-jeebies. I briefly wondered if it belonged to the little girl who'd been killed in the bathroom.

More noticeable than the lack of windows was the two-foot hole in the wall near the floor behind the stairs. The red brick had crumbled and the hole looked like a yawning mouth full of broken teeth opening into a darkened void of a throat. I imagined it was the source of the cool breeze. I passed all the other weathered and worn clutter and headed toward the hole. I carefully lowered my knees to the floor and ignored the bite of dirt and debris as they made contact with the cold concrete and shone the light into the darkness.

The light revealed the inside of a filthy steel pipe large enough for someone to belly crawl through. Cool, dank air hit my face. Water or something had moved or stood in the lower portion of the pipe as there were swipe marks in the dirt and it was slightly cleaner than the top half. I moved the light to the bricks of the opening but didn't see any water lines or residual evidence there had been a flood in the basement. I sat back from the hole and checked the wall of the basement beside the opening.

"What are you doing?"

I yipped in fear and fell back on my ass. I dropped the flashlight and heard the cheap plastic crack and the bulb pop. I let out another terrified sound as the basement was plunged into near darkness. The only light was the faint trickle from the open basement door.

"Jesus Christ!" Brent barked. "You broke the fucking flashlight. That's just what we need. More unnecessary expenses."

I could barely make out the silhouette of Brent standing a few feet behind me. I gripped my chest where my heart hammered furiously. "You scared the shit out of me," I said. I wanted to add the flashlight only cost three dollars at the Dollar General and we probably got our money's worth out of it but bit my tongue instead.

"Yeah, guess so," he said with an air of aggravation. "I'm borrowing the car. I've got an interview with one of the police officers involved with the case."

I patted the ground until I found the broken flashlight and rose to my feet. "Are you taking your laptop with you?"

"Why?"

"I was wondering if I could use it to look for a job instead of trying to read things off the phone. The print is really small."

"As long as you don't fuck with anything except the browser."

"I won't. How long are you going to be gone?"

He sighed. "Don't know. I guess I gotta stop and get another flashlight while I'm out."

EIGHT

THE JOB POSTINGS in the area were dismal. I wasn't expecting anything extraordinary or high paying but most of the job search websites contained the same few postings for fast food joints. Working at a chain fast food place wasn't ideal. I wasn't opposed to working in a fast food restaurant but being forty and working at one put a huge damper on my ego. I passed on all the fast food listings for the moment. If I couldn't find something else within a couple of days I didn't have much of a choice. A job was a job and I needed one. I preferred to work for an independent restaurant where you might be treated like a workhorse but at least you weren't treated like a disposable cog in the machine for the most part, constantly having your job threatened because there was a line of teenagers aching to make enough money to buy whatever it was that teenagers were into these days. But I really wanted to get away from being a server. I was sick of old men trying to save a dollar by swapping out their pollack fish dinner with a piece of cod. Or middle-aged men who bitched about their coffee and then encouraged their teenaged sons to trash the table with open packets of salt and ketchup so they could teach me some passive aggressive message while stiffing me on a tip. And I was tired of greasy and gross ex-cons working in the kitchen hitting on me and putting off a relentlessly rapey vibe.

I began looking for anything that wasn't associated with food. I applied for a receptionist job I knew I wouldn't get even though they touted one didn't need any experience. Even if I did get the receptionist job, I didn't own any business attire and didn't have the money to buy some. I was certain it wouldn't be acceptable to work in a T-shirt and jeans. There were a few pairs of black pants I owned, which were the norm when you ended up working in retail or fast food. And one pair of tan slacks from a previous job that I hated but hung on to in case I ran into another job that required tan pants.

A position for a general employee for a pet store caught my eye. I'd never heard of the place and clicked on the ad to read through the requirements. It was all your standard stuff: high school diploma, hard worker, flexible schedule, etcetera. I checked to see where the shop was located and found it was less than five miles from the house. I didn't want to get my hopes up but I really wanted the job. It paid much better, not a lot, but better than serving tables and relying on tips or working fast food. I didn't know a ton about animals other than the two cats we'd had when I was a kid. Brent was allergic and the funds, time, and space were always too limited to consider any other pet. But I always found if you were willing to work whatever shitty shift everyone else hated and admitted to the employer you didn't know certain things but were willing to learn, some employers were willing to overlook your lack of skills in order to fill the position as long as someone with experience didn't show up and apply.

I finished sending in my application when someone knocked on the front door. I'd been so lost in what I was doing the sound startled me and my heart leapt into my throat. At first I thought about ignoring it. We weren't expecting anyone and I didn't like the thought of answering the door when Brent wasn't home. An occupational hazard of dating Brent meant I'd heard too many home invasion stories. I'd also read too many news sites to not be nervous about a random knock at the door. But then I thought Brent might have scheduled an interview for the book he'd forgotten to tell me about or maybe the landlord was checking in and it was probably best to at least answer the door. It was the middle of the afternoon after all and I couldn't imagine anyone being bold enough to do it in broad daylight or anyone wanting to rob the place after taking a look at the outside of the house.

I made it to the door when the person knocked again. I cursed the lack of a peephole. I opened the door just enough for the other person to see my face and simultaneously braced the door with my shoulder and placed my foot along the edge to keep anyone from shoving it open and barging in.

A thin, clean-cut man with dark hair and translucent skin stood on the porch looking around at the empty boxes I'd stored out there after unpacking. He wore a short sleeve, black button-down shirt and slacks, held a small basket, and appeared close to my age. Maybe a few years older. He turned to me and I had to refrain from slamming the door shut. He had a large scar running down his forehead and cheek and it looked as though whatever had caused the scar had also damaged his eye. It was milky in color and didn't quite sit evenly or move equally with the other. It was a bit alarming. He smiled shyly.

"Can I help you?" I said.

"Hello." He extended his hand. "I'm Dan Miller. I run The Meditation Temple down the road." He tilted his head toward the end of the street where the abandoned looking church was located. After a few awkward seconds of holding his hand out and me staring at it and not reciprocating he finally dropped it. "I'd noticed a car in the drive the past couple of weeks and the plywood had been removed from the windows and assumed someone might've moved in. They normally don't remove the window coverings if they're gonna bulldoze the place. Heck, they don't even bulldoze anything anymore. They just let it all fall in." He proffered the basket to me and I noted it was full of fruit and also contained a small paper booklet. "I brought you a home warming gift."

"Thanks," I said. I reluctantly opened the door enough to retrieve the basket. I thought, *If you noticed a car before why didn't you come when it was here?*

Dan stood expectantly as if he were waiting for me to invite him in. As a woman, you never told a stranger you were home alone. When I was single and a repairman came I always told them my boyfriend would be there any minute, even if they were there for three hours, to keep them on their toes if they planned on doing something terrible. I definitely wasn't going to invite the guy in and he had to assume I was there alone since the car wasn't in the drive at the moment. Alarm bells started going off in my head. He had to know there were only two of us and he had to have seen Brent leave. I could feel gooseflesh rising on my neck and was about to slam the door in the guy's face. He must've recognized something in my expression as he intervened on my horrific downward spiral of thoughts.

"I stopped by to invite you and your family to The Meditation Temple."

"We're atheists."

"Great!"

His response caught me off guard.

He chuckled. "I know what you're thinking. This weird looking guy shows up on your step, offers you a gift, and invites you to some bizarre place. You probably think I'm trying to get you to join a cult."

I wasn't thinking that at all but now that he mentioned a cult I really wanted to slam the door in his face. But his statement about him being weird made me feel guilty, as if I were staring at his unusual eye too much. I opened my mouth to respond but I didn't know what to say.

"It's okay," he said. "I get it all the time. The Meditation Temple isn't a church or a cult. It's a free space for any person of any religion to sit and meditate for as long as they need. The doors are always unlocked and we're open twenty-four seven. Sometimes that meditation involves a person talking to a god or opening their mind for some guidance or answers. There's really no right or wrong way to do it. Some people say it helps with their depression and releases stress." He gave a nervous smile.

The mention of depression piqued my interest. But ultimately, as with anything that sounded interesting, or something I might be into, it most likely came with a price. Anything that sounded too good to be true usually was.

"How much does it cost?" I asked.

"Nothing. I keep a coffee can by the door. It's sorta like the leave a penny take a penny jar you see at a store's cash register. If you feel like donating, feel free to leave what you can. If you need some money, feel free to take what you need. It's not a requirement though. I didn't purchase the place to make money and I'm not an ordained minister or anything. I won't guide you through the meditation. That's something everyone has to do on their own." He nodded toward the basket I was holding. "I gave you a pamphlet all about it in the basket. It also has some recommended books for anyone new to meditation."

I glanced down at the basket. "I'll give it a read when I get a chance."

"Good." He paused. "Well . . . I'll let you get back to whatever you're doing."

I don't know why I offered an answer. "Job hunting."

"Oh, yes. That's got to be difficult. Hard times around here. Especially since Zug Island."

I wanted to ask him what Zug Island meant but decided against it, figuring it was something I could look up later if I remembered the name.

He said, "I assume you're looking for something full-time but if you ever need a few dollars I sure could use someone to tidy up the temple and my living quarters once or twice a week."

I nodded. "I'll keep you mind."

He smiled. "Good. Well, maybe I'll see you around." He turned and exited the porch without ceremony.

I closed the door and made sure to lock it before heading toward the kitchen. I sat the basket on the table and headed toward the window. The curtains were sheer and I watched as he walked toward the old church. There was an air of confidence in his stride but also a bit of awkwardness. His pallor appeared less sickly in the sunlight and I found something I couldn't quite pinpoint stirring within me.

Intrigue?

Maybe.

Attraction?

I felt ashamed to have even considered I might be slightly attracted to Dan. *No*, I thought, *you're not allowed to be attracted to him. Forget him.*

The thought, for some reason, excited me and I found myself hoping he'd turn around and find me watching him. Maybe I wanted anyone who wasn't an asshole or a sleaze bag to pay me a bit of attention. Maybe I needed to try harder to be a better partner to Brent. I felt something vague but familiar surging to the surface of my muddled brain and it brought a bit of clairvoyance. It was like getting a glass full of ice water thrown in your face. That surge of adrenaline. A heaviness in my chest. The teenage longing of lust.

Moments ago I was ready to scream rape and slam the door in this guy's face and now I was pondering my feelings for a complete stranger. What was wrong with me?

I shook my head, as if the motion would clear away my absurd thoughts, and backed away from the window. I turned and spotted the pamphlet protruding from the basket on the table.

NINE

I'D FINISHED HEATING some canned soup on the stove when Brent pulled in the driveway. It wasn't as if I'd slaved over the meal but running the stove had made the kitchen stifling and I pulled the hem of my shirt up to blot the sweat on my face before assembling two peanut butter sandwiches. I'd begun to ladle the soup into bowls and placing everything on the table as he entered the house.

He dumped his notebook and pen on top of his closed laptop and dropped a plastic sack on the table before collapsing onto the chair in front of his meal. I pawed around in the bag he'd brought home and found a handful of battery-powered touch lights, batteries, and another cheap flashlight. I wondered if he was going to place the lights in the basement of if he expected me to do it. I decided to do it after eating even though I loathed the basement. His attention landed on the basket in the middle of the table as I finished looking at what he'd bought.

Brent nodded at the basket. "What's this?"

"A guy from the church down the road dropped it off."

He made a sound halfway between a laugh and a sound of disgust before plucking the pamphlet from the basket. He mumbled something about god and flipped the booklet over to read the back cover.

"I guess it's not really a church. It's a meditation center."

"Oh," he said, raising his eyebrows and feigning interest without taking his eyes off the text. "Even better." He flipped through the pamphlet and gave a smug laugh at some of the text. He laid the booklet on the table and kept turning the pages and began to eat the soup.

Once I noticed he'd reached the area about depression in the pamphlet I spoke up. "He offered me a job."

He kept his head down but lifted his eyes to me. "Doing what? Meditating?"

"His name is Dan. I was looking for a job when he stopped by and I told him, hoping he might be able to point me in the right direction." Actually, I didn't know why I'd mentioned the job search to Dan but the more I talked about the guy the guiltier I was beginning to feel and for some reason I wanted to justify my interaction with Dan to Brent. "He said he could use someone to clean a couple times a week."

"How much does it pay?"

I shrugged. "Not sure. I didn't ask and he didn't offer but it's better than nothing until I can find something else. And I don't need the car to get there so that's a plus."

Brent tossed the pamphlet back in the basket and took a bite of his sandwich. He made no attempt to acknowledge me, what I'd said, or to give his approval or disapproval of the offer, which meant I should do whatever it was I wanted as far as I knew. I thought about asking him what he thought but knew it would be met with the snarky remark of 'do whatever you want.'

I knew what I *should* do and what I *would* do were two different things. And I had to decide if I was willing to be the kamikaze pilot that would destroy everything and everyone around me. You only live once and who wants to be miserable the whole time.

TEN

I CONVINCED BRENT to help me pull the mattress up the stairs and place it in one of the bedrooms so I wouldn't bother him while he wrote and his pecking at the keyboard, his frustrated sighing, and mumbling while he worked wouldn't keep me up at night. But Brent wasn't the only thing that bothered me while trying to sleep. The basement gave me the willies. Even with the door shut. I was certain it was giving me nightmares. Ones where I felt trapped or attacked and helpless with no place to run and no one to help me. I wanted to move the bed as far away from the basement door as possible.

Once the bed was upstairs and I tried to actually sleep I found it was probably a bad idea to move it up there. It was hot even with the windows open and the fan on high. I tossed and turned and found myself fantasizing about Dan, which wasn't bad. For some odd reason thinking about sex sometimes lulled me to sleep. As if counting thrusts was more effective than counting sheep. I wasn't sure what time it was when Brent finally came to bed. I'd dozed off at some point but woke up horny and only tentatively tried to provoke sex from him. He didn't seem interested and I gave up quickly. I waited a few minutes until he began to snore lightly and slid my hand into my panties. Quietly, and with as little motion as possible, I masturbated. I thought about fucking Dan while I did it. There was something dark and mysterious about him and the fantasy somehow morphed into me being fucked on a church altar. The orgasm was so intense it was a struggle to remain still and not yelp with pleasure. Since the hysterectomy, everything had become so sensitive, each orgasm was nearly a whole-body convulsion.

Afterward I lay with my hand still on my cunt and began to slowly drift off to sleep. But once the orgasm had subsided I realized I had to pee. I knew if I didn't go now I'd wake in an hour and *really* have to go. So I wiped my come-covered fingers on the inside of my underwear and pulled on my discarded tank top and shorts. I felt around in the dark until I found my shoes. The last thing I wanted was a splinter in my foot in the middle of the night. Or for someone to pass the house and happen to spot me walking around topless since some of the windows didn't have any covering and the ones that did had sheer curtains. Although the chances of anyone passing the house and spotting me were nearly null since I hadn't recalled ever seeing a car on our street. I hadn't even seen a car pass to go to The Meditation Center since we'd been in the house.

I guess there was more than the heat upstairs that made it inconvenient for sleeping up there. The only bathroom in the house was located on the first floor. It seemed like any house with a second story would at least have a half bath upstairs.

I slipped out of the bedroom and partially shut the door behind me so I wouldn't disturb Brent. The light above the kitchen sink downstairs cast a faint light up the staircase and I slowly made my way down them, trying not to elicit too many loud pops and squeaks from the old wood.

Once I was on the ground floor I noticed the basement door was open and the touch light I'd placed on the wall inside the door was on. I approached the door cautiously. The basement scared me and made me feel childish. I wasn't sure what it was that set me on edge about it. All I could think of was the darkness and the hole in the wall. It felt like a void and a vacuum. There was an overwhelming sense of being sucked into it and never being able to come back. As I got closer to the basement door I could see down the stairs and noticed another light I'd placed at the bottom of the stairs was lit too. From what I could tell, it appeared all of the other lights I'd placed around the basement were on.

I cursed Brent's forgetfulness and knew I had to shut them off. They were battery operated and we couldn't afford to keep replacing the batteries. If I didn't go down there and turn them off I was certain somehow Brent would flip the responsibility on me. Especially if he knew I'd noticed them and didn't do anything about it even though he was the one who left them on. I told myself there wasn't anything to be afraid of and started down the stairs.

When my foot hit the third stair the wood groaned and a large shadow darted across the dirty floor and was accompanied by a scuttling sound. My heart leapt into my throat, and even if I wanted to scream, the fear strangled my vocal cords. The terror froze me in place. They say the natural defense mechanism to a threat is flight or fight. Not me. I always froze up like a statue. I had an opossum defense. I shut down at the first sign of conflict. This also held true to verbal confrontations. My friends used to call me 'the door mat.'

I only realized I'd been holding my breath once I started to see black dots swimming in my periphery. Slowly, I let out the breath I was holding and took another, trying not to make a sound. I listened but didn't hear anything. I wasn't sure what to do. I didn't want to go down there but I also knew I wouldn't be able to sleep if I didn't make sure no one was in the basement. The best solution was to arm myself before descending into the basement and hoping, if there was a person down there, they didn't have a gun. For a moment I thought of waking Brent but deep down I knew I was being paranoid and the last thing I wanted was to be scolded in the middle of the night for 'imagining things' and having the situation blamed on not taking my medication.

I quietly retrieved a knife from the kitchen and began to descend the stairs slowly. The stairs popped and creaked and I knew there was no way I'd be able to keep silent. The house was too old and rickety to attempt to be stealthy. Once I passed the clearing of the upper floor I ducked down and leaned my head over the stairs to get a look at the basement. There was no one down there. I stared at the hole in the wall for at least a minute, waiting to see if anything emerged. I don't know what I was expecting but nothing happened. The fear of what may or may not be down in the basement put more pressure on my already full bladder and it was becoming painful. I stilled my nerves and dashed down the stairs. As quickly as possible I shut off all the lights and ran back up the steps, shutting the stair lights off as I went. I had to stop myself from slamming the basement door once I reached the first floor.

When we first arrived I'd noticed the sliding lock on the outside of the basement door and found it peculiar. Why would anyone ever feel the need to lock the basement door in such a fashion? Did someone need to restrain someone in the basement? But now, as I stood bracing the door shut against an invisible threat, I knew why. I flipped the lock and wondered who else had been terrified of the basement.

I took a step back from the door and felt slightly safer. I started to wonder if my mind wasn't running full force with my fears. I swore a shuffling sound came from the other side of the door.

My bladder couldn't take any more.

I dashed to the bathroom with the knife still in my hand and dropped it on the counter. I hadn't noticed I'd been sweating profusely until I tried to shimmy my shorts down. I dropped my shorts in time for my bladder to let go. A half groan escaped me involuntarily as I urinated. When I was finished and done washing my hands I splashed some cool water on my face and stared at my features. The bags under my eyes were dark and my eyes seemed expressionless. I looked dead inside. I dried my face with a towel and vowed to avoid looking at myself as much as I could help it.

I felt exhausted and my mouth was dry. I cautiously opened the door and started toward the kitchen, unable to take my eyes off the basement door, listening for any sound. I didn't hear anything else and headed toward the sink. I grabbed a glass from the cabinet and was about to turn the tap on but thought better of it. I hated the way the tap water tasted and knew the gross taste of sleep in my mouth would only make it worse. I had purchased some juice the other day and thought it a better option.

It took a few seconds for my mind to register what I was seeing after I opened the refrigerator door. I dropped the glass and it shattered on the kitchen floor. I was glad I'd voided my bladder as I would've pissed my pants had I seen this before.

A hunk of unwrapped meat sat on a plate in the middle of the refrigerator. Meat I hadn't purchased. Meat that bizarrely looked like a heart. It was sitting in a puddle of blood and the coppery and menstrual stench of the blood made me want to gag. My mind raced to put it all together. Why would Brent go and buy such a thing? What was he thinking? There was no way in hell I was eating it and there was no way in hell I was going to cook it. Who the fuck eats hearts? What kind of animal was it from? It looked big. Like a pig heart or something.

I knew, whatever the reasoning was for him purchasing it, that he'd spent money on it and it was a waste. But for some reason I became angry. I snatched the plate from the shelf and stormed toward the back door. I had half a mind to take it upstairs and dump it on his head while he slept in order to wake him up so I could tear into him about wasting our money on some pointless food item I would neither cook for him nor eat.

When I reached the back door I had to slam my hip into it while trying to balance the slippery organ on the plate before the door finally flew open and slammed into the side of the house. I tossed the organ out into the dry, brown grass of the backyard, spilling blood all over my hands and forearms, which made me even angrier with Brent.

I returned to the kitchen and washed the plate and my hands while I fumed. I cleaned up the broken glass and I couldn't wait until the morning when Brent noticed the damn meat thing was gone.

At that point I was no longer tired. I had no idea what time it was as the phone was plugged in upstairs. I knew I wouldn't be able to sleep if I returned to bed and I found myself in the kitchen, mindlessly searching the food in the fridge and the cabinets, looking for any other surprises Brent might've ran out and bought while I was asleep.

I turned from the fridge and cabinets and spotted the meditation pamphlet lying on the table. I retrieved it and spotted the bold box declaring 'open 24/7' and dropped it back on the table.

ELEVEN

THE NIGHT AIR felt thick and damp against my skin. There was no breeze and the insects were singing their hearts out and the sound was almost deafening.

I checked the sky for any sign of morning light but there was nothing. No moon. No clouds. Only a speckling of stars one could see amidst the light pollution of the city. There were no working street lights on our road and I wondered if I would be able to see the stars at all if they'd been working.

I remembered the stars from my childhood as I stared at the night sky. When I was eight my parents drove me to Vermont to stay with my aunt and uncle over summer vacation. My aunt was a homemaker and didn't mind the company and it was a way for my parents to enjoy their summer without me around and to not have to find or pay a sitter. My aunt and uncle lived in a tiny cabin on the side of a mountain, miles away from any city. Uncle Jonathan would come home late in the evening and sit outside on the deck after dinner and drink beer and smoke cigarettes. My aunt would extinguish most of the cabin's lights and retreat to the sitting room located on the opposite side of the cabin to work on her knitting. I would join Jonathan and the both of us would watch the night sky, occasionally catching a shooting star. It was the first time in my life I realized how many stars there really were and how small I was in comparison to life in general. Without the light pollution the night was pitch black and it was as if you could see the whole universe.

A dog barked in the distance and snapped me out of my reverie. A mosquito buzzed in my ear and I swatted it away before I started toward the meditation center. Although there were not street lights on our road there was a light at the intersection to the main road. It was dim and barely cast any light down the street. I took to walking down the middle of the road as I couldn't recall if the sidewalk ran all the way to The Meditation Temple or not.

A soft glow came from the stained-glass windows of the transformed church, a mashup of blue, green, yellow, and orange. It wasn't clear from this distance what images were meant to be displayed but it didn't matter. Even if I could see the images clearly I didn't know anything about Christianity and wouldn't be able to identify what was depicted in the glass.

For some reason I began to feel anxious as I approached the building. My vision began to swim some and it wasn't until I was hit with a bit of dizziness that I realized I was holding my breath. I took a few deep breaths and tried to collect myself. Why was I getting so nervous about entering The Meditation Temple? Because of Dan? *No*, I thought, *you're not coming down here because of Dan. Get that out of your head right now. You need a job. You need to try meditation as a medication replacement. There is nothing nefarious about your visit. You're mad at Brent and you need to calm down.*

I thought about turning around and heading home but some

contrarian part of me refused to stop or go back. I had the same mindset as a teenager. Always stubborn. Always refusing to relent. I thought of the murder house as if it were my childhood home. I couldn't go back there. I was on my own now. Just like the first day after moving out from my parents' house. Occasionally I'd drop back in for a visit and it was awkward and I had the sense I wasn't welcome there anymore. The feeling never went away. Even after they both died and me and my brothers were forced to clean out their house. The murder house didn't want me there either and I knew it.

My eyes finally adjusted to the poor lighting and I could make out The Meditation Temple better. There was one car parked in the retired church's lot. I spotted the sidewalk and followed the path to the main entrance of The Meditation Temple. The stained-glass of the two doors depicted a violent scene and seemed like a bizarre juxtaposition for a place promoting serenity. I pulled the handle of the door gently, expecting it to be locked regardless of what the pamphlet claimed, and found it opened easily and soundlessly. The place didn't look dilapidated but I'd anticipated a loud groan of old hinges and a harried stare from someone attempting to meditate. Neither of which happened.

I found an air-conditioned and empty room with a coat rack housing only bare coat hangers. The floor was covered in worn maroon carpet. To the left was a set of steps leading up to another set of doors and to the right was a hallway. The first door in the hallway had a 'Ladies' sign affixed to it at eye level. I turned toward the stairs and noticed a second set of steps descending beside them. I peered down the second set of stairs but there were no lights on down there and something about the darkness made me shiver. I told myself it was the air-conditioning and climbed the first set of steps.

Before entering the doors I spotted a short table with a coffee can sitting on top of it. There were a few crumpled bills in the can. Dan had mentioned it was a 'take or leave' can. I thought about taking everything, cramming it in my pocket, and leaving, but I felt guilty taking all of it and decided I might take a dollar or two before leaving to make up for Brent's grocery splurge.

I pulled one of the doors open, anticipating a creak, but found this set as soundless as the first. There was no one in the room and there was a familiar scent I couldn't quite place. The door made a deep knocking sound when it shut behind me.

I'd entered the former sanctuary and the silence once the door was shut was a physical thing and was suffocating. I imagined the former church had soundproofed it. I wondered if all churches soundproofed the area where they held their sermons to keep from pissing off the neighbors. All the pews had been removed too. In their place were several large white pillows, the type one would use to sit on the floor, and their contrast against the maroon carpet appeared almost sickly. The pulpit was void of any furniture and there was a faint dusty outline of a cross up on the wall. There was something about the removal of such a vital religious item from the former church I found funny and had to stifle a laugh. The giggle fit made me realize exactly how tired and slap-happy I was.

I strolled down the makeshift aisle, scanning the pillows, as if I were going to spot one that was any better or softer than the others by looking at them. They were all the same and I picked one at random before sliding my shoes off and sitting on it. My joints protested as I lowered myself to the ground and it was moments like this I knew I was getting old. I did what I could to get comfortable sitting but gave up quickly and grabbed two other pillows and lined them up before lying on my back. The pamphlet had recommended sitting in a lotus position but ultimately encouraged whichever position was most comfortable for the person.

I folded my hands over my heart, closed my eyes, and focused on my breathing like the pamphlet had suggested. After a couple of minutes my body began to feel detached from the pillows I was lying on and I started having a sensation I was flipping end over end and suspended in weightlessness. I wasn't sure if what I was doing was correct but I embraced the sensation of uncontrollability and let my body spin out of control and out into the universe, into the billions of stars and the void of everything. I became weightless. I became unthinking and receptive.

I didn't dwell on things that normally plagued me. Mainly death. And how I was going to die. Was that a palpitation? Death by heart attack. I hope it's quick. Why does my side hurt? You get cancer. Where is Dr. Kevorkian when you need him. Is that bus going to hit me? Winner, winner, chicken dinner. You get to die in an accident. Quick and painless.

It was all gone. No thoughts. No worries. Nothing. Nothing. Spinning and weightlessness and the void.

I became the void.

I am nothing.

I am everything.

I am a part of it all.

I am a part of nothing.

Deeper.

Deeper.

Dark.

Darker.

Black.

Nothingness.

Void.

Spinning, spinning, spinning.

Something pulled me back and I shot up to a sitting position, gasping for air. I was confused and disoriented and dizzy. My body was damp with perspiration. I wiped the sweat from my forehead and was struggling to assess whether I'd fallen asleep or not when I noticed I wasn't the only person in the room.

Dan, dressed in all black again, was sitting on a pillow near the door at the back of the room. He was sitting in a lotus position with his hand resting on his knees as if he'd been meditating. Apparently my outburst had disrupted him as he was staring at me with a crooked smile.

My embarrassment did nothing to stanch my sweating. I pulled on my shoes and looked to the stained-glass windows to see if the sun had begun to rise yet. There appeared to be some faint sunlight outside but I couldn't be completely sure. My knees popped when I rose to my feet and my hips and lower back felt stiff as hell. I did my best not to limp as I headed toward the door, avoiding making eye contact with Dan. I knew I needed to talk to him about a job but I was almost certain I'd fallen asleep and felt embarrassed. I didn't want him to think I'd come down here to sleep like a homeless person. My lower back began to loosen up. The first ten or fifteen minutes after waking up were the only time I felt this stiff and since going off the antidepressants every ache and pain felt magnified by a hundred.

Dan spoke up as I neared him. "Good morning."

"Mornin'," I said. I ran my hands through my hair nervously. "Sorry, I didn't mean to fall asleep. I couldn't sleep and thought I'd give it a try." I felt my face flush.

He chuckled. "Happens to the best of us. No need to be embarrassed." Dan rose to his feet. "Sorry, I don't think I caught your name the first time we spoke." He extended his hand.

I shook his hand quickly. "Laura Dyer."

"Were you interested in the job?"

"Cleaning?"

"Yes."

I looked around the room, trying to assess what would need cleaning. The place was worn and a bit outdated but it didn't look dirty.

"It may seem like a big job but it's not really. I run the vacuum late at night when no one is here, take out the bathroom trash daily and scrub them once a week, and I spritz the pillows with an essential oil spray twice a week."

I nodded, realizing the spray must've been what I smelled when I entered the room.

"Sandalwood," he said.

"I was trying to put my finger on it."

"I used to use lavender but . . ."

"Too many people fell asleep?"

He smiled, tight-lipped, as if he were trying to hide his teeth. "Modern stresses take their toll on people. It's not uncommon for someone to get so relaxed they fall asleep. Sleep can be the most relaxed state of mind one can be in provided they're not troubled by nightmares. You can learn a lot about yourself in sleep."

"Like dream interpretation?"

"Yes. Among other things. You can learn to control your dreams through lucid dreaming."

"What's that?"

He opened his mouth to say something but lifted a finger to his lips and tapped it in contemplation. He dropped his hand. "I have a book I'd like for you to have. Follow me." He turned toward the door and looked back to me once he reached for the handle.

I wasn't thinking of much other than he was about to lead me somewhere more private and I wasn't sure if I should follow him but something about my expression gave him pause.

"It's fine," he said. "It'll only take a minute. I'm sure your husband won't mind."

"Boyfriend."

Dan smiled and nodded. "I won't keep you much longer."

I followed him.

We left the former sanctuary and he turned to descend the dark stairs. I hesitated at the top and once he was halfway down he stopped to look up at me. Something about the complete darkness raised gooseflesh on my arms. Something about the shadows cast across Dan's face made my heart race.

He raised a hand to me. "Sorry, I don't turn the lights on in the hall to deter people from exploring down here. I know the place like the back of my hand so I don't need the light."

I took his hand reluctantly. It was warm and dry and felt stronger than he looked. After a few steps I did detect a slight tremor in his grasp and I couldn't be sure if it was me or him.

At the bottom of the stairs we walked forward about ten feet before turning left. I held onto Dan and ran my hand lightly along the wall to keep myself from feeling disoriented in the dark. I couldn't judge the distance but in front of us I could see a sliver of light shining from a crack under a door.

There was a vague odor I couldn't put my finger on. Something familiar. The farther we walked the more pronounced the smell became. It wasn't until we'd almost reached the door with the light that it dawned on me that the smell was exactly like the smell emanating from the hole in our basement. Once we reached the door Dan let go of my hand and opened it.

He motioned for me to enter. I stepped into a studio basement apartment lit by a lone lamp with white walls and white bookshelves overflowing with books. Stacks of books lined the walls as well. There was a futon for seating, a small television, a record player with speakers and a couple of milkcrates with LPs. Nothing was hung on the walls and there was an overpowering smell of incense. A folding privacy screen did a poor job of hiding a full bed and dresser in one corner and on the opposite side of the room there was a kitchenette. I imagined the door beside the kitchenette was the bathroom.

"Cozy," I said.

Dan passed me and headed straight for a tome in a stack on the floor. He retrieved a book and flipped it to the back before handing it to me. The book was titled *The World of Lucid Dreaming*. Brent would think the title dumb and I laughed.

Dan gave me an uneasy smile. "Something wrong."

I waved dismissively. "Nothing. My boyfriend is an author and a little opinionated about books. I was imagining what his reaction to the title would be."

"An author?" He sounded excited. "That's fantastic."

I made an uneasy sound. "It's not as glamorous as you think. Most people's perception of authors and how they live comes from outdated television shows and movies. There was a time when authors received ridiculous advances but now they're lucky to get enough money to live off of for six months."

"Really?" He seemed genuinely shocked.

"Yeah." I flipped the book over to read the description.

"Is the neuroticism the same as the movies?"

I laughed a little too hard. "Like you wouldn't believe." I focused on the back cover again.

He said, "Lucid dreaming is when the dreamer is aware they're dreaming and can control what happens. They can even wake themselves up if they're having a nightmare."

"Whoa. That's crazy. Do you lucid dream?"

He nodded. "I discovered it by mistake. I knew I was able to wake myself up if the dream became too frightening but I had no idea that it was something people tried to teach themselves until I discovered that book in my early twenties. Sleep paralysis, REM sleep disorders, Exploding Head Syndrome. They're all things people strive for in order to discover things from their subconscious self."

"Exploding Head Syndrome? That sounds terrifying. Is that like a stroke?"

He gave me a crooked smile. "No. Some people will hear a loud noise as they're drifting off or right as they wake up. A bang or clang or, in my case, a loud electrical zap."

"Terrifying."

"I guess one's self could be terrifying to some."

I waved the book at him. "Thanks for the book. I'll bring it back once I'm done."

"No problem."

We both stared at each other awkwardly. I could feel my face begin to flush again and my eyes began to dart around the room, trying to avoid looking at him. A twinge of arousal pulled at my sex.

He said, "Would you like a bottle of water? It's not tap water."

"No. I'm fine," I said. "Yeah. The tap water is gross."

His expression became grave. "Don't drink the tap water. Don't ever drink the tap water."

His sudden change in demeanor was unsettling. "Okay. Yeah."

"The pollution from Zug Island has settled into the ground and the water is contaminated."

Oh, god. A conspiracy theorist, I thought. *Great.* I didn't have much patience for conspiracy theorists. I would humor them but I couldn't buy into whatever mental disorder they had that made them paranoid and delusional about things that clearly didn't exist. Did this guy really believe the drinking water was polluted and the city or government hadn't done anything to fix it? Who could afford to buy water when it was free from the tap? Or at least free from the tap because the publisher was paying for our utilities.

"Okay," I said.

His expression softened and he thankfully didn't pursue the topic any more.

"Well, I should get home." I started to say 'before Brent wakes up' but found I didn't want to bring up Brent in front of Dan anymore. I wanted to pretend Brent didn't exist around him. My brain was screaming 'You idiot! What are you doing? You can't do what you want to do! Forget about him!' but there was an undeniable pull when Dan was around.

"Sure," he said. "So are you interested in the job?"

"Oh, umm . . ."

No! No! No! Don't take the job. This is bad. You know it's bad. You're going to want to fuck him and it's all going to end badly because you have no impulse control and especially when you're off your meds.

But we need the money and no one has responded to my emails or applications.

That's a poor excuse. You know something will come along. Just give it some time. Don't you love Brent? You know where this will lead.

Are you kidding me? This doesn't have anything to do with needing a job, does it?

I need a job. We need money.

We?

Yes.

But you really don't give a fuck about Brent.

How can you say that?

Because if you truly cared about him you wouldn't even consider putting yourself in a situation in which you KNOW you will want and at least attempt to be unfaithful to him.

Unfaithful? That sounds religious. I'm not religious.

You don't have to be religious in order to care whether or not you break someone's heart. Someone you love.

"Laura?" Dan looked concerned.

"Yeah? Sorry, just thinking."

"Were you interested in the job?"

TWELVE

THE SUN WAS barely hidden beyond the horizon when I left The Meditation Temple. The birds had begun to sing and a few of the stars were still visible. I found myself humming and without prompt I sung a few lines in a whisper.

"*And I'm floating in a most peculiar way. And the stars look very different today.*"

I continued to hum as I walked back to the house, thinking, *I'm digging my own grave and happy as a lark. What the fuck is wrong with me?*

But reality came crashing back down on my head as soon as I took a step onto the porch. And the clarity of my situation slapped me in the face once I was in the house and headed toward the kitchen.

Brent was sitting nude at the kitchen table, typing furiously. A cigarette was perched in the corner of his mouth and he had one eye squinted against the smoke as he typed. Something with a sickly yellow hue was smeared across his chest and a second later the stench hit me and my stomach rolled. Under normal circumstances I would leave him alone. Normally if I interrupted him while he was writing it would end in an argument. But this wasn't normal. Brent quit smoking almost ten years ago. He'd never written in the nude. And by the putrid smell filling the kitchen and competing with the cigarette smoke I was certain the yellow sludge smeared on his chest was bile.

"Brent," I said timidly.

He didn't stop or acknowledge me.

"Brent," I said with more confidence.

Still no response.

I approached the table, stood beside him, spoke his name again, and he still feverishly typed away. I took the opportunity to read what he was writing:

And then I vomited. She has to be poisoning me. I will only be eating food I prepare from now on. Something about this house has changed her. There is an overwhelming presence I can't explain but I know it's here and it has infected her thinking. She disappeared in the night and I believe she's being absorbed into the house and feeding off its malevolence or possibly feeding it by committing evil acts.

I'd read enough. I slammed the book Dan had given me on the table and barked, "Brent!"

He started and the cigarette fell from his lips and landed in his bare crotch. Brent shot to his feet, knocking the chair over, and began swatting at his penis while shouting incoherently. Once he spotted the smoldering cigarette on the floor he retrieved it and extinguished it in a cereal bowl on the table which I hadn't noticed before but was filled with at least a half a pack of butts. How long had he been at this?

Brent glared at me with his finger still smashed against the dead cigarette.

"What are you doing?" I asked.

"What are *you* doing?" he responded.

"I couldn't sleep so I decided to check out The Meditation

Temple. Thought it might help relax me. Might help since I'm out of antidepressants."

He guffawed. "Yeah. You need a lot of help."

I pointed at the laptop. "What the fuck is this?"

"The truth."

"The truth?"

He crossed his arms over his vomit-streaked chest. "Yeah."

"You think I've poisoned you?"

He didn't respond. Only stared at me with a hateful expression.

"You're out of your fucking head. That's why you bought that heart or whatever the fuck it was?"

"Ain't that the pot calling the kettle black. Out of my fucking head? What are you talking about?"

"The heart. In the fridge. The one I threw in the backyard!"

"I have no fucking clue what you're talking about."

I stormed to the backdoor and slammed into it to get it open. I walked out into the dew-covered grass and looked for the heart in the area I was certain it had landed. There was a spot of bent and broken grass and some dried blood but the heart was gone. I stomped back into the house and found Brent in the kitchen where I had left him. He had a confused look on his face.

"I don't know what you did with it," I said, "or if a stray dog took it but you know what I'm talking about."

"Holy shit. You need to go back on your meds."

"Me?! You're buying animal organs to eat and accusing me of poisoning you!"

"Are you fucking high?!"

I snatched up the pack of cigarettes sitting on the table. "Ten years!" I shook the pack at him. "Ten years and you decide to smoke half a pack in one sitting. You don't think that's what made you sick? Get a hold of yourself." I flung the pack in the direction of the trash can. It hit the wall and bounced to the floor.

Brent eagerly retrieved the pack and fingered the flip-top lid as if it were something precious I might've broken. "Where were you?" he hissed.

"I told you. I went to The Meditation Temple. As a matter of fact, I spoke to Dan afterward and got a job cleaning the place. So, you're welcome. We'll now be able to afford groceries and your fucking smoking habit. But as far as I'm concerned you can fix your own fucking meals from now on."

"Fine."

I grabbed the book off the table and turned to retreat to the bedroom but stopped and turned back to him. I looked at the computer for a second, took a deep breath to calm myself, and said, "I can leave if you want." I nodded toward the laptop. "Doesn't sound like you want me here anyway."

I don't know why I'd said it. I didn't have anywhere to go. The car was his. How the fuck could I leave? There was a sick part of me that wanted Brent to tell me to go. If he told me to get out that meant I wasn't at fault for ending the relationship. If Brent told me to leave that meant we were officially over. But another part of me wanted him to beg me to stay. I wanted him to apologize for some manic episode he'd had or sleepwalking or . . . I don't know. Something. I wanted him to be panicked and frantic at the thought of me leaving. I wanted him to at least act like he still loved me.

He said, "Do whatever you want. I don't care."

His words felt like a physical blow. It felt as though he'd sucker punched me in the gut. I don't know why. Hadn't I known for a long time he didn't really care about me anymore? It was like when a woman would ask her friends if they thought her husband was cheating on her, rehashing all the vague evidence of infidelity. If you're asking if your partner is cheating on you, don't you already know? If you're asking, it's because all the signs are right in front of your face and you're in denial. I was in denial that Brent still cared about me. He didn't give a fuck. All he cared about was himself and his fucking writing. Those two things were the only things on his list of priorities.

Well, fuck him. He only kept me around to make his life more convenient and I wasn't going to be his mommy anymore. He was on his own. He could cook his own food, clean his own dishes, wash his own clothes, clean up after himself. I wasn't doing it anymore. I guess I could walk out on him and be done with it but I wanted to stick around and make him miserable. I wanted him to hurt the way I was hurting at that moment. It seemed only fair. How long had he been wasting my time? How long had he known he didn't give a shit about me?

I wanted to hurt him the way he'd hurt me. I said, "You smell like a sewer and it's making me sick. Clean yourself up, fucking hog." I didn't give him a chance to retaliate or reply. I spun on my heels and stormed off to the bedroom to get some sleep before I started my new job that night.

THIRTEEN

CLICK CLICK . . . CLICK click click.

A faint echo of an erratic beat filled the darkness and suddenly I found myself walking without knowing where I was or how I'd gotten there. I was in the middle of an empty and decaying city and there wasn't a person to be seen. None of the cars moved. Everything was still.

Click click click click . . . click.

I tried to match my stride with the sound but it was impossible. The tempo was too frantic. I began to notice a presence, or a lack of presence, coming from behind me. I turned to see a crumbling cliff at my heels and nothing but space and a void behind me. The distance into the nothingness made my stomach hurt. For every step I took forward the world previously under my feet had crumbled away and fallen off into space. The end of the world was right behind me.

I began to run.

Click . . . click click . . . click click.

I ran through the empty streets of an unfamiliar city as the world disintegrated behind me.

I ran and ran and ran without ever getting winded and it felt like running through molasses. I ran to the edge of the city and looked back to see nothing but darkness. I ran through the countryside as fields behind me were devoured by the void. I ran through small towns and past campgrounds.

Click click . . . click click click . . .

I ran past farms and restaurants and stores. I looked back and they were eradicated. I ran through deserts and over mountains. I ran past lakes and schools. I ran down highways.

Click click . . . click . . . click click.

I ran to the beach and stopped. A sharp drop into nothingness behind me and the tide touching my toes in front of me. The tide running up over my shoes. The tide running up over my ankles and dropping off the cliff and into the void. The world was gone behind me and the tide was coming in.

Click . . . click . . . click click . . . click.

The tide came up to my shins and I struggled to keep my balance and stay standing. The tide receded. In the distance a large swell rose higher and higher, coming closer and closer. The wall of water was taller than me and it was gaining speed.

Twenty feet away.

Fifteen feet away.

Ten feet away.

Five feet—

I gasped and shot up to a sitting position in bed. The book Dan had given me fell to the floor. I'd fallen asleep while reading it. I gulped air and squinted against the early afternoon sun. An overwhelming sense of relief washed over me as the realization it was only a dream settled in. I was sweating profusely and the sheets were damp.

The box fan did little to relieve the stifling heat as the sun was shining directly on me through the bare window.

The clicking of Brent's laptop echoed through the house. The bedroom smelled heavily of cigarette smoke and made it difficult to breathe.

When we moved the bed upstairs I'd noticed there was a curtain rod above the window but no curtain. It wasn't an issue before. We went to bed once it was dark and were up once the sun rose. It had been a long time since I'd had to work a night shift. I'd forgotten how difficult it was to get sleep during the day while the rest of the world was awake. Thankfully we didn't live on a busy road or near any businesses. I recalled the time I worked in a shitty factory and lived in an apartment above an elderly couple's garage and how the damn neighbors would put their fucking dog out on a chain, regardless of the weather, at nine in the morning and left it out there until nine at night and the fucking thing barked nonstop. I always wanted to get an airhorn and stand outside the neighbors' bedroom window and blast the thing every three seconds from nine at night until nine in the morning on my day off so they could see how fucking annoying it was when you were trying to get some sleep.

I got out of bed and went to the closet where we kept the boxes with our clothes and bedding. I found a blanket and proceeded to gingerly drape it over the flimsy aluminum curtain rod, hoping the weight of the blanket didn't break or bend the hooks holding the rod.

Once I'd blocked the majority of the sunlight from roasting me I returned to the bed but stopped when I spotted the book on the floor. The book had fallen open to an illustration of a sleeping woman draped over a bed. A demon-type creature was perched on the woman's stomach and a faint horse with glowing eyes was in the background. The description read 'The Nightmare' by Henry Fuseli. I picked up the book and flipped to the index in the back until I found the word 'water' and turned to the page listed beside it and read:

Water occurs commonly in dreams, as it's a universal symbol for emotions.

Turbulent waters will appear in your dreams when you are in an emotional crisis. You may dream later that you're crossing the same waters but they are calm once the crisis has passed. Raging waters may be a symbol of self-discovery while a flood or a tsunami are there to remind you to let go.

I closed the book and laid it on the floor. I got into bed and lay on my back. I draped my arm over my eyes and mumbled, "Tell me something I don't know," before trying for more sleep. I hoped it was dreamless this time.

FOURTEEN

THE HOUSE WAS quiet when I woke later in the evening. I lay in bed for a few minutes listening for any sign of Brent but my grumbling stomach and full bladder forced me out of bed. When I stepped out into the hallway I found the attic ladder was down. I called for Brent as I approached the ladder but there was no reply.

A light was on in the attic. I placed my foot on the first step and tested the rickety thing. I knew the moment I got halfway up it I wouldn't be able to get much farther but with the way Brent had acted earlier I wouldn't put it past him to give me the silent treatment. The last thing I wanted to do was to accidently shut him up in the attic. As much as a small, smug part of me would love to lock him in the attic overnight I didn't want to have that argument. I definitely would never hear the end of it. Years would pass and out of nowhere Brent would feel compelled to throw it in my face again to make me feel guilty.

I took a deep breath to steady my nerves and began to climb the ladder, hoping my bladder would hold out. *It's only a few feet,* I thought. *You're not going to die if the ladder breaks.* I focused on the ledge of the opening and tried not to let the bending and shifting of the old wood freak me out. My palms began to sweat and I forced myself to keep going. Once I'd made it halfway up my bladder really began to protest. It wasn't until I'd made it to the top that I thought I should've brought the cell phone with me in case I did fall and break my leg and piss my shorts.

I grasped the edge of the opening with a death grip and peeked over the edge. "Brent?"

He wasn't in the attic. The attic was nearly empty. There was a trunk and what looked like an old 8mm projector sitting on the lid. A sheet was hung on the wall as a makeshift screen and the projector was pointed at it.

I gave myself a small pep talk and tried not to think about how far off the ground I was or how full my bladder was and pulled myself into the attic, scraping my shin savagely in the process. I sat on the dirty wood floor and cursed as I assessed the missing skin and trickle of blood running down my leg. Once I'd gotten all the fucks and cocksuckers out of my system I turned my attention back to the projector.

I walked cautiously across the attic, wondering how safe it was to be up here. The floor was constructed of old, unfinished particle board and was swollen and warped in several places. It was apparent the roof leaked and the attic floor took the brunt of the abuse. I noticed some fresh, deep scratches in the flooring as I neared the trunk. It looked as though Brent had dragged the trunk across the floor. I followed the scratches as they led to a makeshift door in the wall.

The door was merely a piece of plywood with a hole drilled in it as a handle. There were no hinges. The whole door popped out of the wall when I stuck my finger in the hole and pulled. It was difficult to see without the flashlight but it looked as though someone had stored their holiday decorations in the makeshift closet and either forgot about them or didn't give a shit about leaving them when they moved. I put the door back in its proper spot and went to investigate the trunk.

The projector had film in it and was plugged in. I lifted the projector off the trunk and set it on the floor. The trunk's latches were rusty and difficult to open. Inside were some Christmas ornaments and an empty space I imagined was where the projector was stored. There was one box for a reel of film but it was empty.

I closed the lid and put the projector back on top of the trunk before looking it over. There was a switch on the top and I flipped it. The projector started and the film began to turn but no picture showed up on the sheet. I looked the contraption over and found another switch labeled 'lamp' and flipped it. A grainy, dim picture appeared on the sheet. I made my way to the overhead light and pulled the cord to shut it off. The attic was plunged into darkness. The only light came from a small window on the front side of the house.

In the film, the cameraperson was walking through the house. The house was in much better condition than its current state and held furniture that appeared outdated but in good shape. The cameraperson began climbing the stairs. For some reason, watching as they ascended the stairs caused me to break out in gooseflesh. They appeared to be creeping along as if they were attempting to keep quiet. And there was something about the scene that made me think it was happening directly below me in real time although it was apparent the film came from another time period. Once the person was at the top of the stairs they panned to our bedroom.

The door to our bedroom was open but the room was outfitted with a four-poster bed. Someone was sleeping in the bed. The cameraperson approached and got close to the person's face. It was an older woman with dark hair. Her mouth was slack and her eyelids twitched as if she were dreaming. The cameraperson didn't move. They kept her sleeping face in frame. I wasn't sure how long the camera lingered on the sleeping woman but it was becoming uncomfortable. Suddenly, the camera jerked up and the cameraperson exited the room hurriedly. The picture became a jerky mess as the person made their way down the stairs. The person stopped in the living room and directed the camera to the open basement door. There were no lights on in the basement. The camera was focused on the blackened doorway. The frame shook in such a way I imagined the cameraperson trembling. I watched closely as something moved in the doorway. I couldn't tell what it was. The picture and doorway were too dark but I swore it might've been a person. The picture disappeared and was replaced by some weird markings and then the picture went white. The film began ticking as it flipped against the projector. It was done.

I turned on the overhead light before shutting the projector off. I needed the reassurance of the light because the film had creeped me out and had made me very aware of how badly I needed to pee. I could feel the trickle of blood from my wounded shin sliding down my leg and the sensation intensified my urgency to relieve my bladder.

I shut off the overhead light and slowly began the terrifying descent down the ladder. Once I made it to the bottom I closed up the attic door and dashed down the stairs, heading toward the bathroom. Just as I made it to the living room Brent opened the front door, holding a grocery sack. I'd been so focused on getting to the bathroom that his sudden and unexpected appearance frightened me and I screamed. My outburst frightened Brent. He jumped and looked at me like I'd grown a second head.

I continued hurrying toward the bathroom and called, "Gotta pee!" Brent murmured something about me being a psycho as I slammed the bathroom door. As I was relieving myself I realized the kitchen knife was still on the bathroom counter. I looked to the shower and couldn't help but think of the Hitchcock movie.

FIFTEEN

I'D USED ALL the Band-Aids we had left on my shin after exiting the shower. I'd forgotten to bring any clothes with me so I wrapped myself in a towel and slipped my shoes back on. When I finally opened the door of the bathroom I was assaulted by a foul smell I'd never encountered before. I was certain it was something Brent was cooking but I had no idea what it was and I hoped it was something he wouldn't cook anytime in the near future. The stench almost made me gag and as much as my stomach had been grumbling I wasn't sure I'd be able to eat, even if it was something entirely different. I resigned to the idea of making a sandwich and eating it on my way to work so I wouldn't have to smell whatever it was that Brent had made.

I found Brent in the kitchen, scraping the last bit of something from a pot and into a bowl. An opened can of Dinty Moore Beef Stew sat on the counter. I thought about making a remark about how

I didn't think what he was cooking would be any less poisonous than whatever he thought I was feeding him but I kept the snark to myself.

The evening breeze coming through the window was cooler than normal and the wind was picking up. I peeked through the sheer curtains in the kitchen and spotted a line of dark clouds in the distance and two flashes of lightning. It took several seconds for the faint rumble of thunder to be heard.

"Great," I said to no one in particular. "It's going to storm."

Brent didn't respond.

I headed toward the bedroom to get dressed. I dug through several of the boxes in the closet until I found my jeans. I wasn't sure if the storm was bringing in a cold front but the temperature of the air coming from outside seemed to be dropping drastically by the minute. I got dressed and continued to root around in the boxes until I found my rain jacket. The Meditation Temple wasn't far but I had no idea how long the storm would last and I didn't want to get soaked.

I shut the bedroom window before heading back down the stairs and found Brent typing on his laptop with one hand and spooning the last of the beef stew into his mouth. A strong wind whipped the kitchen curtains around wildly. Brent didn't seem to be concerned with the coming storm so I dropped the rain coat on the back of my chair and closed the window before I proceeded to make a peanut butter sandwich to take with me. I was hungry but the smell of Brent's rotten canned dinner still hung in the air and I didn't think I could eat it now.

When I was done wrapping the sandwich I turned to him and leaned my hip against the counter. I said, "I shut the attic."

Brent stopped typing and looked at me as he swallowed the last bite of his food. I waited a few seconds for him to say something but he stared at me expectantly. I wasn't sure what he was waiting for but his expression looked slightly worried.

"It was open when I woke up," I said. "I went up the ladder to see what was up there."

His eyes narrowed the tiniest bit as if he were suspicious or possibly confused.

"I watched the movie up there."

He furrowed his brow and said, "What movie?"

"On the projector."

He shrugged his shoulders. "What projector?"

"The one you drug out of the hidden closet. God, Brent, I swear you're trying to fucking gaslight me."

"Laura ... I honestly have no fucking clue what you're talking about. I'm not fucking with you. There's nothing in the attic except for the mousetraps I put up there."

My heart skipped a beat. If Brent didn't pull the trunk out of the hidden spot then who did? Was there someone else in the house when I was sleeping?

"Okay," I said. "I'm going to be one-hundred percent honest with you right now. I'm fucking scared."

I turned to look up the stairs. Everything looked normal. I turned back to Brent. He had followed my gaze and then met my eyes. A flash of lightning lit up the kitchen window followed by a loud crack of thunder that made me jump.

He spoke slowly. "What's going on?"

I tried to remain calm. "I woke up and found the attic open and the ladder down. I climbed up there because the light was on and I wanted to turn it off. When I got up there I found a trunk had been dragged out of a makeshift hidey place and a projector was sitting on top of it. There was a movie roll in the projector and I watched it. The movie was sorta creepy. I'd shut up the attic and had to pee and was headed to the bathroom when you came home. I figured you'd been up there going through stuff when I was sleeping and ran out for something."

Fat drops of rain began to fall on the kitchen window pane.

His eyes widened. "I wasn't up there. I didn't find any projector." He stood abruptly and headed for the stairs.

"No no no." I followed him and grabbed his arm to stop him. "Don't go up there. What if someone *is* up there?"

"I think we would've heard them by now." He tried to pull his arm from my grip.

"Call the police. Have them look first."

The rain began to pelt the roof.

He turned fully toward me and sighed. "To be completely honest with you, I think you're full of shit."

I let go of his arm and took a step back as if he'd stung me. "What are you talking about?"

"You accuse me of gaslighting you? I think you're either fucking with me or you need to take some of the money you make tonight and see a doctor to get back on your meds. There's no trunk up there. There's no hidden door. There's no movie."

I folded my arms across my chest. I was done. I wasn't going to argue with him. I was going to wait for him to climb the ladder and see for himself. I might struggle with depression but I wasn't schizoaffective.

He turned back to the stairs and climbed them. I followed him and stood back as he lowered the attic door. I stayed in the hallway while he went into the attic. The light came on and Brent was gone less than ten seconds before he started back down the attic ladder.

He looked at me and waved his arm to insinuate I should take a look for myself.

The fear of heights didn't even cross my mind. I bolted up the ladder and looked over the edge. The trunk was gone. "What the fuck?" I said and climbed onto the attic floor. Not only was the trunk gone but there were no scratches on the floor and there was no hidden door in the wall.

Am I losing my fucking mind?

I rubbed my forehead for a moment, trying to process what had happened. Water was starting to drip in a few spots on the ceiling. My mind struggled to find the logic in what I'd seen. I thought, *Okay.*

Bitch, you need to see a doctor.

    I turned off the light and descended the ladder. Brent waited in the hallway. I didn't say anything to him as I closed the attic door. When I did turn to him he looked very stern. As if he were about to discipline a child for lying. I felt as though I were a dog being punished for shitting on the floor. I couldn't make eye contact with him and passed him without a word and headed down the stairs. I needed to get to work.

SIXTEEN

IT WAS HARD to tell if the darkness was all from the storm or if some of it could be attributed to the setting sun as I walked through the downpour toward The Meditation Temple. My mind felt jumbled as I tried to piece together what had happened. Had I been asleep? That wasn't possible. I had a horrendous scrape on my shin from climbing into the attic. How would I have gotten that if I'd only dreamed of finding the trunk in the attic? And the movie on the projector ... How and why would my mind have made that up? If I hadn't been in such a hurry to leave the house I could've looked up the imagery in the dream book to see what it had to say. I'd wanted to get out of the house and away from Brent as quickly as possible. I'd left in such a rush I almost forgot my coat and sandwich.

I tried to clear my mind as I walked. The last thing I wanted was to come off as aloof on my first day of my new job. Not that cleaning required much brainpower or focus but, still, no need to make Dan second guess his decision to hire me even if it was all under the table.

Thunder rumbled in the distance and I looked up at the sky. I had no idea what time it was and Dan and I hadn't agreed to any set time or day. He told me I was free to set my own hours. I assumed it was okay to pop in whenever I wanted to work since the place was open all the time. I figured the night shift was the best because I hated being in the house at night since it gave me the creeps and it was more likely there would be fewer people meditating at night.

As I approached The Mediation Temple I took notice of an older minivan parked in the lot. Someone was meditating. Dan hadn't given me any instructions on what to do if people were actively meditating. He hadn't even shown me where the cleaning supplies were.

I opened the door and made sure to hold it as it closed so it wouldn't make any noise. There was an umbrella propped against the wall beside the coat rack but other than that the place looked exactly the same as the last time I'd been there. The rain created a steady sound as it beat on the roof but the volume was less deafening than in the house.

I figured the meditation room was off limits so I hung my wet jacket on a hanger as soundlessly as I could, leaving my sandwich in the pocket, before I made my way toward the stairs leading to Dan's living quarters. I cursed myself for not bringing the phone or at least a flashlight I could use once I got to the bottom of the stairs. The same thin line of light shone from the bottom of Dan's door down the hallway and I felt along the walls as I made my way toward it. Once I made it to the door I could hear some music being played softly inside.

I felt a cool, stale breeze coming from farther down the hall and thought I heard a shuffling. I held my breath and listened and swore I could make out a faint sound. It almost sounded like a sigh or breathing.

A thunderclap startled me. I didn't want to be in the hallway anymore. I tried to rap on Dan's door lightly but hit it with too much force.

Dan opened the door with a worried expression. A haze of incense smoke hovered behind him. He wasn't wearing a shirt, socks, or shoes, only a black pair of linen pants with a drawstring waistband. Before averting my gaze I noticed several scars on his chest. A couple of them were crescent shaped.

"I'm sorry," I whispered. I pointedly stared at the ground. "There was someone meditating and I wasn't really sure what I needed—"

Dan stepped back abruptly and turned but left the door open. He snatched a black T-shirt from the futon and pulled it over his head quickly but not before I noticed more scars on his back. I could tell from his movements and posture the scars were either a source of embarrassment or something he didn't care for other people to see.

He turned back to me with a nervous smile and said, "It's okay." He motioned me in. "Come in. You can wait in here for a bit."

"I didn't mean to interrupt you."

"It's no problem. Really. Have a seat."

I felt my face flush as I stepped in and shut the door behind me. "I'm really sorry I—"

He waved a hand to cut me off. "If I didn't want people to bother me I wouldn't have made the place accessible twenty-four hours a day." He motioned for me to take a seat on the futon. "Do you want some water?"

"Uh, yes. Thank you."

He retrieved a bottle of water from the refrigerator before taking a seat on the opposite end of the futon. He nodded to my ankles. "Got a little soaked."

I looked at my pants as I removed the twist cap from the bottle of water and took a sip. I'd been so wrapped up in what had happened at the house I hadn't paid much attention to whether or not I'd tromped through a million puddles on my way here. Not only were my pants soaked but so were my socks and shoes.

"Guess so," I said. I let out a nervous chuckle before looking around his living quarters again. I found myself staring at a corner near the ceiling for too long.

"Everything okay?" Dan asked.

"No. I mean yeah. I'm fine." Dealing with depression was exhausting and one could only keep up the façade for so long before you started to crack. People who were observant could always tell when something wasn't quite right. There was one excuse I'd found that worked no matter what because it was also a partial truth when a bout of depression hit. I said, "Just tired."

"Didn't sleep well?"

"Not really. Something weird hap—" I stopped myself. *What was I doing? I couldn't tell him what happened. Get your shit together, Laura.*

Dan looked at me expectantly. "Something weird?"

I shook my head. "The house is creepy. That's all. Keeps me from getting any sleep. Figured it would be better to work at night to get away from it. It doesn't bother me so much during the day. It's going to take me a while to get adjusted to the new sleep schedule."

He nodded. "That's understandable."

The music that was playing softly came to a stop. A soft pop came from the speakers and then a small click sounded from the record player as the needle dropped back into its proper place. Dan stood and retrieved the record from the player and slipped it back into its cardboard sleeve before replacing it in one of the milkcrates.

He turned to me. "Any requests."

"Play whatever you like. I'll listen to anything." I took another drink of water and replaced the cap before setting the bottle on the ground by my feet.

He chuckled. "I sorta have a strange taste in music. What do you normally listen to?"

I shrugged. "Whatever is on the radio. I don't own any records or CDs or anything. It always seems like everyone around me has specific tastes so I let them pick. I don't care much for country though."

"Not a fan of country myself." He pulled a white album from one of the milkcrates. I'd never seen the artwork before and it was very minimal. He placed the LP on the record player and the music that began was somehow a mix of electronic, atmospheric, instrumental, and new age. I'd never heard anything like it but could see how someone could easily meditate or fall asleep to it.

He grabbed one of the milkcrates and sat it in front of me before he took a seat beside me. He said, "You're more than welcome to take off your socks and shoes and give them a chance to dry." He pointed to the crate. "Pick a record."

I removed my socks and shoes like he suggested before carefully flipping through the records. Touching people's music always felt extremely personal and made me nervous. When I was twelve or thirteen I'd gotten a job babysitting and I'd spent the majority of my money on CDs and cassette tapes. One of my brothers had taken it upon himself to go into my room when I wasn't home and take whatever music or money he could find. Of course I was pissed about the missing money but I took even more umbrage with the theft of my music. Music had been an escape for me then. Back when depression was an ugly word and you'd thought I'd told my parents I worshipped Satan instead of trying to ask for help. I learned real quick to keep my feelings and problems to myself unless I wanted my parents to threaten to have me 'committed.' I didn't know what that all entailed but I'd seen *One Flew Over the Cuckoo's Nest* and I sure as fuck didn't want to have a lobotomy. Back then the lyrics from bands like The Gits and Mudhoney called to me in a way that said 'you're not the only miserable sack of shit on the planet.' I took solace in music back then. Now I found comfort in antidepressants and I was out of those.

I found an album with a photo of a pretty, young blond girl on the front and pulled it from the milkcrate. "Who's this?"

"Chromatics."

"Never heard of them."

"They're dream pop. Kinda synth pop."

"I think I might be too old to listen to them."

"Nonsense. Here." He held out his hand for me to hand the LP over.

He replaced the album on the player with my selection. I could see why he called it dream pop once the girl began to sing. Dan watched me for a reaction as I listened.

"I like this." I waited a beat. "A lot. It's soothing. Not as chaotic as some stuff."

He smiled as he stood in front of the record player. It was as if he'd been waiting to rip it from under the needle if I hadn't liked it. He returned to the futon. We both sat without speaking, listening to the music. I leaned back and my eyes landed on Dan's lap. A wave of embarrassment washed over me when I noticed he had an erection. My face flushed and my cheeks tingled and I diverted my eyes, hoping he hadn't noticed I was looking at his dick.

I stared at the door as my mind raced. I wasn't completely sure his arousal was because of me but I'd wished I hadn't looked. Why had I looked? My heart sped up and I shifted forward and sat on the edge of the futon. I was about to tell him I was going to check to see if the person meditating had left when Dan leaned forward also. He reached under the futon and retrieved a small wooden box. I recognized the box for what it was once he spoke.

He said, "Do you smoke?"

The question was so far out of leftfield it left me speechless for a few seconds. "Oh. Uh . . . I used to. It's been a really long time. Like, a decade. Maybe longer. I smoked a lot of pot in high school to cope."

"Cope?"

"I wasn't very popular. Got picked on a lot. I used it as a coping mechanism."

He lifted the box to me. "Would you like to? I promise it's only pot. It's medical. Certified and everything."

"I probably shouldn't. I don't think I'll be much good if I get high. I'd probably spend all night vacuuming the same spot over and over."

He chuckled. "Okay. You don't mind if I do, do you?"

"No. Go right ahead."

Dan opened the box and retrieved a dugout. I felt like I was visiting some artifacts from a former self. *God, how long had it been since I'd seen a dugout?* He flipped the top of the contraption and the fake cigarette popped up. He pulled the device from its home before mashing it down in the other slot for the pot. He grabbed the lighter next to the incense burner before he lit up.

The smell took me *way* back. It instantly brought back a memory from high school. Sitting in the back of Tom Jacobs' car in a wooded area where the local teens went to make out. Getting high and kissing. A lot of heavy petting and two horny teens trying to fuck while stoned out of their heads. I had such a crush on Tom but no matter how hard we tried to fuck in the back seat of his car it wasn't meant to be. We were both so nervous. He had a hard time keeping an erection and my cunt locked up tighter than Fort Knox. It wasn't until years later that I discovered what vaginismus meant. I was so heartbroken back then when Tom didn't return any of my calls afterward. Back then I thought there was something horribly wrong with me and that was the reason we weren't able to fuck and why he stopped seeing me afterward. I never dated another guy the rest of high school. I was terrified Tom had told everyone. Knowing what I knew now I realized he was probably more embarrassed than I was over what had happened. What teen guy wanted his peers to know he couldn't get his dick up?

Dan breathed out a cloud of smoke before saying, "You okay?"

"Yeah. The smell brings back some old memories."

"Good ones I hope."

I held out my hand, indicating I'd like to take a hit. "Can I?"

"Sure."

"You don't have to pay me for tonight. Let's call this hanging out."

"We'll call it orientation. I'll show you where everything is afterward. And the office."

I took the littlest hit I could and blew it back out immediately. It had been a long time and I didn't want to get too high because I knew that would make me paranoid. "There's an office?" I handed the one hitter back to him.

"Yeah," he said. "That's where the closet with all the cleaning stuff is. It's down the same hall as the restrooms."

I sat back on the futon and closed my eyes as the pot kicked in and listened to the music. My whole body began to tingle and I felt weightless.

I said, "I guess this stuff would really enhance meditation."

"Among other things," he replied.

A roll of thunder shook the place.

I wasn't sure exactly what he meant by the statement but my mind warped it into something sexual. I became instantly aroused. I felt the futon shift as he put the wooden box back under it. I squeezed my eyes shut tighter as if that would keep me from thinking about his erection or keep me from peeking to see if he was still aroused. My hand was on the futon beside me and I felt what I thought were his fingertips brush mine as he laid his hand by his side and leaned back. His finger twitched beside mine and there was no mistaking what was happening here. He did not move his hand so that it wasn't touching mine.

This was an invitation. I didn't have to accept. I could ignore it and act oblivious. I'm sure Dan would pretend he meant nothing by it. But the spark of desire was pulsing within me. There was something alluring about Dan. I was certain it was the old cliché of mystery. There was a story behind the scars that called to me. There was pain there. Physical and mental. He had gone down a very fucked up and crooked path in life. One no one could ever understand. Just as no one could ever understand what it was like to deal with depression unless they'd walked that very same mile.

I had to make an excruciating decision now. Get up and go home to a man I knew no longer loved me and didn't seem to be remotely attracted to me anymore or stay here. I didn't want to go home. What would Brent say if I came home high as fuck and with no money? I couldn't imagine the argument that would follow and sure as hell didn't want to do it while stoned. I could stay here and not do anything. Just talk. Just be friends with Dan or, better yet, let him be my boss. Nothing more. God, I was so high. And there was no reason to make any stupid decisions at the moment.

For fuck's sake. It was only his finger touching mine. Why was I making a huge deal out of it?

Because you want him.

Doesn't matter. I'm in a relationship.

Are you really though? Or are you just a convenience? Someone to bring home some money. Maybe a hole to fuck every once in a while.

His fingers slowly slid the tiniest fraction over mine.

Fuck, I thought. *You know you can't be friends with him. And remember . . . this is all your fault.*

I slid my hand from under his and slowly up his thigh. I opened my eyes to look at him. He had his eyes closed and his head leaned back. He opened his eyes and looked at me. His expression was indecipherable and each second felt like an eternity because of the pot. I began to panic. Maybe I'd misread his signals. Was I making an ass of myself? Maybe he wasn't interested in an unemployed forty-year-old woman. Maybe he had better morals than I and wasn't about to fuck a woman who he barely knew but knew well enough to know she was in a long-term relationship.

All of that melted away when he leaned toward me and ran his hand in my hair to pull me into a kiss. I could taste the pot and metallic one hitter on his tongue. The rest happened quickly and violently. Both of our breathing became heavy as we kissed. I ran my hand over his stiff cock. He groaned and pushed his pelvis against my hand. I began to pull at his shirt but he grabbed my hand to stop me. I pulled at the tie strings of his linen pants. He ran his hand under my shirt and over my bra. He squeezed my breast hard and I yipped even though our mouths were still locked together.

I broke from the kiss and almost ripped my shirt as I pulled it off and removed my bra. Dan began to suck on my nipples and bite them. My arousal soared and my cunt began to soak my panties. I tugged at his waistband again. He pulled my hands away from his pants.

"Please," I said.

He unfastened my pants in response and pushed me to lie down on the futon. He pulled my pants and underwear off inside out and tossed them on the ground. He placed a hand on each of my knees to spread my legs. I tried to grab at his pants again.

Whenever I got drunk and fucked the act of fucking seemed to sober me up. Not the case when I was high. It made me clumsy and slow and I never sobered up.

Dan thwarted my efforts to disrobe him. He shot me a devious smile before he lowered himself to bury his face in my cunt. This definitely wasn't his first time at the rodeo and it had been so long since I'd been the receiver of oral attention that my orgasm came quick and hit like an earthquake. I squeezed my thighs around his head to keep from smashing my pubic bone into his nose when I bucked from the first intense wave of orgasm. I couldn't help but yell in ecstasy. The pot made every sensation more razor-sharp.

When the orgasm subsided Dan rose to his knees and wiped at his mouth with his forearm. I flipped over and got to my hands and knees. Dan took no time lowering his pants now and entering me from behind. I reached between my legs and spanked my cunt hard as another sharp wave of pleasure soared though my body and I begged him to fuck me. He grabbed my hair and yanked my head back. I couldn't help but laugh. He fucked me furiously and shouted when he came.

We both collapsed on the futon to catch our breath. After a few moments he pulled his pants up and retied the waistband. I grabbed my panties from the floor and slid them on to keep from leaving a wet spot on his futon. We lay there in silence for a few moments and I realized the music had stopped playing.

This probably should've been the time I was flooded with regret. But I wasn't. And the fact that I didn't feel bad about being unfaithful to Brent sorta made me feel bad. The situation and my feelings were a hundred degrees of fucked up.

He said, "What are you thinking?"

"I don't remember pot making me so horny."

He laughed. His laughter was contagious.

SEVENTEEN

I STILL WASN'T able to coax Dan out of his clothes when we had sex the second time. It was obvious he was self-conscious of the scars. I didn't bring it up. Even in the aftermath when I lay against him and ran my hand over his chest and traced the scars through his shirt.

Dan was aggressive and authoritative during sex which I didn't mind. He knew what he wanted and he wasn't afraid to tell me. I'd had enough of the other person only doing what needed to be done for them to get off and nothing else. The sex felt animalistic and as if he needed it to survive. I felt wanted and crucial.

Neither of us brought up the obvious in the aftermath, that I'd cheated on Brent. It was something I would have to figure out on my own. And hadn't I already made up my mind about leaving him before leaving the house. I just wasn't sure how I was going to end it. It had to be quick. I wasn't sure how long I could stay in the house after being unfaithful. It would eat at me. And there weren't enough degrees of separation between Dan and Brent. I wasn't exactly sure how Brent would deal with the separation. Brent had never been a jealous person and he'd made it painfully obvious he wasn't interested in being with me anymore but the stress of change could make a rational person do stupid things. And asking Dan if I could move in shortly after fucking was jumping the gun a bit. I decided discussing Brent or moving would ruin the mood so I didn't say much of anything. Dan remedied the awkwardness by choosing to show me where the cleaning supplies were once we got dressed.

I figured we'd been downstairs long enough that the person who'd been meditating should've left by now. But when we reached the top of the stairs the door to the meditation room opened and a plump woman, who appeared to be in her seventies, emerged. She wore a long loose dress with a vague flower pattern. Her hair was long and she wore several beaded necklaces. She gave off a hippie vibe and smiled deviously at us as she descended the stairs.

"Have a good session?" Dan said to her.

"Oh, yes," she said. "Sounded like the two of you had a good one too."

My face flushed and I could only imagine my horrified expression. I wished the mortification would sober me up but it didn't. I was still high and at a loss for words. I wanted to run back down the stairs and hide but I turned to Dan for an answer. He suppressed a smile and looked at the ground as he tried to hide his own embarrassment after being overheard.

The woman laughed. "No need to be embarrassed." She waved at us dismissively. "Sex is a natural thing. It's also great medicine for stress and headaches." Luckily she didn't shower us with any more wisdom and retrieved her umbrella before stepping out in the rain.

Dan took the steps two at a time and opened the door to check the meditation room. He descended the stairs and said, "We're the only ones here."

"She heard us," I said. It was the only thing I could think of to say.

"It's okay."

"I thought this place was soundproofed."

"The walls are. Not so much the floor or the ceiling of the basement."

I laughed and tried to suppress a fit of giggling.

"What?" he said.

"Just makes me feel like a teenager. Like getting high and covertly fucking in the basement when your parents are watching television upstairs or asleep. Guess we should've been quieter."

He smiled. "Guess so." A beat of silence passed before he added, "Let me show you the office."

The rest of the night we went over the cleaning schedule and supplies. He showed me the office past the restrooms. It was small with a plain metal desk and the closet he promised. He helped me clean by spraying the pillows while I vacuumed the meditation room. When we were done cleaning for the night and the first few shades of sunlight were beginning to show we headed back to the office to put everything away. This led to another round of heated sex, this time on the desk. He took his time but I was so full of lust and the remnants of the pot made everything so intense that I came in no time.

There was a bit of awkwardness when we finished. Neither one of us knew how to end the night. He eventually took a seat behind the desk. He opened one of the drawers and retrieved an olive-green metal box and set it on the desk before opening the lid. He began counting some money and I suddenly felt cheap.

He held the money out to me. "Is a hundred enough for a day's worth of work?"

"I, um . . . I can't take that."

He shook the money at me. "What are you talking about? You cleaned. This is your pay."

"It sorta makes me feel like a prostitute."

He set the money on the desk, rose, and came to me. He placed his hands on my shoulders and looked into my eyes. "Don't ever think of yourself that way. And don't ever think of me as the type of person who would pay for sex. I've been perfectly content with masturbation."

I snorted a laugh. The pot was almost entirely out of my system but it was still making me slaphappy. He smiled but forced a serious expression after.

"I don't know," I said. "You helped me."

"It was orientation. I was showing you. Besides, I didn't have anything else to do."

Before I could respond he grabbed the money off the desk, folded it, and crammed it into the front pocket of my jeans.

"Don't argue with me," he said. He left his fingers in my pocket and pulled me toward him. He crushed out my protests by shoving his tongue into my mouth.

I wanted to tell him no. I wanted him to take the money back. I was so happy and content around him and being paid for it felt a hundred shades of wrong. I wanted to remind him that the money wasn't only for me but for Brent. I wasn't comfortable with any of it but decided to let him have his way. And my arousal at his touch cleared all the bullshit from my brain and I couldn't think of much other than fucking.

Eventually he pulled away and I knew I had to go home. Dreaded home. He walked me to the door and watched as I pulled on my coat and left without another word. I put my hand in my pocket and found the peanut butter sandwich I'd forgotten to eat. I ate it while I walked through the rain, racking my brain for how I was going to deal with Brent.

EIGHTEEN

BRENT WAS STILL asleep when I arrived home. The bowl he'd been using as an ashtray was half full and the table was scattered with empty cigarette packs and ashes. The house smelled like a stale bar and I found several empty beer cans in the trash.

I headed straight to the shower to clean off the sex and cleaning grime before placing the stopper in the tub and filling it with hot water. I reclined so that only my face was above the surface and closed my eyes. I mindfully began to relax all my muscles and tried to become weightless. The world became mute with my ears submerged in the water and all that I could make out for sure was the sound of my breathing. I began to walk through the steps to meditate, focusing on my breathing and keeping it in a steady rhythm.

Reality began to fall further and further away as I sank into the void, looking for answers. How should I deal with Brent? Should I tell him I was leaving as soon as he wakes up? Should I wait until he finishes his book? If I left now where would I actually go? It would be presumptuous to show up at Dan's door with what little possessions I had.

This isn't meditation. This is dwelling on the possibility of dreadful outcomes.

I forced myself to clear my mind and float. I reveled in the contentment and afterglow of good sex. As much as I wanted to equate how I felt to a cat basking in the sunlight I actually felt more like a snake that had finished gorging itself. I wanted to curl up in a warm dark place and sleep for a few days, avoiding the inevitable turmoil ahead.

As much as I tried to meditate I couldn't focus and found myself replaying the sex I'd had with Dan over in my head. I grew aroused and masturbated before exiting the tub. I wrapped myself in a towel, slid on my shoes, and made my way to the bedroom. The storm had cooled the house considerably and I shivered as I climbed the stairs. Brent was snoring softly and for some reason the sound grated on my nerves. I hoped he woke up soon because I wasn't sure if I'd be able to sleep with his snoring and honestly I didn't want to share a bed with him.

As quietly as I could I rummaged around in the closet and found a clean shirt, underwear, and pajama pants and pulled them on. I slipped into bed without disturbing Brent and surprisingly fell asleep within minutes.

I dreamed I'd finally had enough money to go to a doctor. I told the doctor what prescriptions I took previously and described how I'd involuntarily stopped taking them since I didn't have any money to refill them. The doctor listened to me the entire time with a smarmy expression and when I was done explaining everything they told me they weren't going to write the prescription and it was all in my head. The dream took a hard left at that point and the doctor began to preform invasive tests that were completely unnecessary. He performed a pap smear and probed my anus, telling me my prostate was fine. I tried to fight the doctor off once he began to rub his erection against my ass but, like in most dreams, I was too weak to fight.

I woke up sweating profusely and my heart was racing. The sun was trying its damnedest to break through the blanket I'd hung over the window. I had no idea what time it was but it appeared it had stopped raining. The confusion coming out of sleep was staggering and I thought the doctor was still trying to molest me but partially came to my senses and realized it was Brent rubbing his erection on my ass and groping my breast. The transition from the dream to waking left me foggy-headed and nothing from the night before came to mind.

I scooted away from Brent, shut my eyes, and muttered, "I'm sleeping."

"Come on," he said. "I'm sorry. Let me make it up to you."

I buried my face in my pillow and groaned. Brent pulled at the waistband of my pajama pants and I smacked his hand away as the reality of what I had done with Dan came back to me.

"Come on," he whined.

I turned to him and barked, "Would you leave me alone?!" I flipped back away from him.

He cursed under his breath and flopped onto his back. A few seconds passed and the bed began to shake. I didn't have to look to know what was happening. He was masturbating. I pulled the pillow over my head and wished he'd hurry up and finish so I could go back to sleep, or at least try to sleep.

After a few minutes Brent grunted and the bed stopped shaking. Another minute passed and he finally got up and went downstairs. I got out of bed and shut the door so I wouldn't hear him going about his day. Or at least the noise would be muffled. And I tried to get some more sleep because I knew I was going to have to tell Brent tonight that this was over.

NINETEEN

BRENT IGNORED ME when I entered the kitchen. I'd been in such a daze I'd forgotten to put on shoes before coming downstairs. My teeth were still grimy from sleep and I could only imagine what my hair looked like. Not that any of that mattered. I didn't need to be presentable for the conversation I was about to have and I wanted to get it out of the way.

Brent was preoccupied with staring at his laptop. His expression was blank and he appeared lost in thought. It was the first time I'd noticed the dark circles under his eyes and it appeared he may have lost some weight. It made me feel a bit guilty. I'd been so wrapped up in my own bullshit I'd failed to pay attention to Brent. He was usually neglectful of his hygiene when he was pressed by a deadline but it looked as though his health was taking a toll this time. I imagined the chain smoking and binge drinking had a little to do with his appearance. I took a seat across from him and waited for him to acknowledge me.

"We need to talk," I said.

He gave a half-hearted laugh. "Yeah."

I didn't hesitate. "We're over. I thought about waiting until you'd completed the book, afraid the emotional toll would affect your writing. But I'm pretty sure you don't give a shit about me and haven't for a while so you'll probably find this as a relief."

Even though I knew he didn't care I was expecting some sort of reaction. Anger maybe? Or possibly an apology. It didn't matter. I had made up my mind and I tensed for some type of reaction but it never came.

His expression didn't change. "How am I going to buy food?"

It took a second for his question to sink it. It wasn't the response I'd expected. "Wow," I said flatly. "It's one thing to think someone doesn't give a shit but it's another to know it. You don't give a care that I'm leaving. You only care that you won't have any money."

He shrugged.

"Well," I said, "I was going to tell you I wasn't going anywhere fast since I don't have a car and I only have one day's pay . . ." I pulled the cash from my pocket and tossed it on the table. "Keep it. It's all you're worried about anyway. For my own mental health I think it would be better if I move out."

Brent retrieved the money and counted it, unashamedly.

"I'm moving into The Meditation Temple as soon as I discuss it with Dan."

He folded the money and stuffed it into this pants pocket. "That weirdo?"

"You've never even met him."

"I've seen that scrawny Johnny Cash wannabe motherfucker skulking around down there."

His ridicule of Dan angered me. "You don't know the first thing about him." It came out with more venom than I intended.

Brent scrutinized me for moment. "Are you . . ."—he squinted—"Fucking him?"

Even I didn't believe the dismissive sound I made. I couldn't deny it though. And did I really want to deny it? It was a surefire way to make sure Brent and I were over. As much as I'd love to make Brent feel bad by telling him Dan was a better fuck and had a bigger cock I didn't have it in me to kick him while he was down. I'd just told him it was over. Dan wasn't something I wanted to discuss with him at the moment and was hoping to avoid the conversation until a later time.

"Don't bother answering. You're a terrible liar," he said.

My face grew hot and I stared at a glass of water sitting next to his laptop. I couldn't bring myself to look at him. It was true. I'd always been a terrible liar and I hated doing it.

He laughed without humor. "Hope he enjoys how frigid you are. And so you know"—he leaned forward as if he were going to divulge something conspiratorial—"you're a lousy lay and I fucked around on you more than once." He sat back, crossed his arms over his chest, and smirked at me.

I knew he wanted to tear me down and make me feel like shit. I couldn't blame him. If I were in his situation I'd be petty and hurtful too.

I said, "This is how it's gonna go, huh?"

He shrugged and continued to smirk. There was something in his eyes that I recognized. He was lying. I wasn't sure if it was about me being a lousy lay or that he'd fucked other women or both. It didn't matter either way.

"Okay," I said. "I think we're done here. Keep the money. It'll be the last you see from me." I couldn't help but take a jab at him. "Maybe you can finally get a real job and stop pretending to be a writer."

I stood, turned, and hadn't taken two steps before something flew past my head, hit the wall, and exploded. Water and broken glass showered me and the kitchen. It took me a couple of seconds to realize Brent had thrown the glass of water at my head. I turned and gave him an incredulous look. There was a gleam of delight and viciousness in his eyes.

"Satisfied?" I asked.

He shrugged. "Not really."

I'd had enough. It was apparent he was going to be childish about the situation. I turned and took a step. A sharp pain erupted behind my big toe. I sucked in air and lifted my foot, knowing I'd stepped on a piece of glass. It was a large chunk too. I pulled it from my foot and blood began to drip onto the floor almost instantly.

"Fucking great," I hissed. I turned back to him and briefly thought about throwing the bloody chunk of glass at his head but decided that would only escalate the whole thing into more physical violence. I threw the shard at Brent's laptop. It hit the back of the open screen and bounced to the floor.

Brent shot to his feet and knocked his chair over. "What the fuck?!" he barked. He closed the laptop and inspected it for any damage. "Fucking bitch! If you break my laptop I swear to god I'll break your face!"

I carefully made my way to the bathroom, avoiding any more broken glass and tracking blood through the house. I wasn't sure how I was going to bandage the cut. We were out of Band-Aids.

Once in the bathroom I sat on the edge of the tub and turned on the water. I put my foot under the faucet and pried open the cut to rinse it out. It burned like hell but I had to make sure it was clean. I wasn't sure if it needed stitches but, by the looks of it, I was sure it did. I put the plug in the tub. I figured it might keep it from bleeding so much if I submerged it in water.

I cut the water once it was to my ankle and yelled at Brent, "Bring me the superglue!"

"Get it yourself, you fucking cunt!"

"You fucking did this, asshole! Now bring me the fucking

superglue!"

I heard him stomping around and slamming the kitchen drawers. Every place we lived we always designated one of the kitchen drawers as the 'junk drawer.' It was our makeshift tool box. It was where we kept the hammer and screwdriver along with random items like superglue and batteries and whatever random things we might need. The sound of crunching glass was followed by heavy footfalls coming toward the bathroom.

I was staring at the pink bath water when a tube of superglue hit the wall above my head and landed in the water.

"Would you stop throwing things?! Ya fuckin' maniac!" I turned toward the doorway but he was already gone.

A hand towel was on the counter and I grabbed it. I spotted the kitchen knife on the countertop and started having some horrendous thoughts. I shook my head and pulled my foot from the water and pressed the towel against the cut, trying to stanch the blood.

A strange noise came from the kitchen and I didn't pay attention to it as I tried to stop the bleeding. Once the bleeding had slowed I took the opportunity to glue the wound shut. I wasn't sure if it would hold but I thought there was some electrical tape in the junk drawer. If I could get it to stop bleeding long enough to grab it. I sure as hell wasn't going to ask Brent for anything else. The sound coming from the kitchen grew louder and what I thought at first was Brent sweeping up the mess was starting to sound like something completely different.

I stopped blowing on the glue, trying to dry it. I called, "What are you doing?"

The sound stopped for a second before resuming at a quicker tempo. Maybe the acoustics were off but it sounded as if he were slurping soup. The closer the sound came to the bathroom the more certain I was that Brent was slurping soup or a drink or something. I figured he was doing it to get on my nerves.

"Would you knock it off?" I said. "Stop acting like a child."

The sound stopped. The floorboards creaked as he retreated back to the kitchen.

I touched the glue to make sure it was dry and let go of the skin, hoping the wound wouldn't open back up. I was still afraid to put any weight on it until I'd wrapped it in tape.

The front door closed as I was rinsing the blood out of the tub. Good. I wouldn't have to deal with him. I could make out the car starting and pulling out of the driveway as I used the bloody hand towel to mop up the blood in the bathroom. When the bathroom was clean I went to take care of the other blood I'd tracked through the house since I knew Brent wouldn't clean it up. But other than a smear right outside the door there wasn't any other blood. How could that be? I knew I had to have left a trail. I could see smears and cleanish spots where the blood should've been but there wasn't any blood. Maybe Brent had cleaned it up. In the reflection of the light I spotted what appeared to look like hand prints on either side of one of the spots in question. I squatted down to get a closer look.

My mind must be playing tricks on me again, I thought.

The more I looked at the spots the more it looked like a dog had licked the floor. I felt the hairs on the back of my neck rise and shivered involuntarily. I didn't care if it was a trick of the light or a trick of my mind. It was time to pack my shit and leave.

TWENTY

DAN LOOKED UP from the book he was reading and gave me a curious look when I walked into his living quarters. I'd stuffed all my clothes and toiletries into two giant boxes, stacked one on top of the other, and carried them down the street to The Meditation Center. I'd had to pull on a hoodie as the wind itself felt cool and I could tell the change in the season was upon us. The boxes had wanted to slip against the fabric of the hoodie covering my arms. Maneuvering down the steps and through the darkened hallway had been a bit of a challenge. I could feel my face flush in embarrassment when I dropped the boxes in the middle of Dan's living room.

I stammered, "I-I'm real sorry. But I put an end to me and Brent and I don't have any place to go. I know this is sorta soon but I can sleep on the futon or in the office and work a few days to get some money to find my own place—"

He closed his book and stood. "It's okay."

Even though he said it was okay I could detect a touch of reluctance in his expression. Here was this sad woman uprooting her entire life and forcing her way into his house after one day of fucking. I knew if a guy did that to me I would have been extremely hesitant. I would feel like my life was being encroached on. How long had he been living as a bachelor? Maybe he preferred living on his own. Maybe he didn't want to have a 'girlfriend.' I know if I was living on my own, fucked a guy, and the next day he showed up with all his belongings, I would think he was unstable.

"I'm sorry," I said. "I don't want you to think I'm one of those crazy girls who move in on your life and take over. Me and Brent have been done for a long time and he's been acting strange lately and I didn't feel safe."

Dan's expression became concerned. "Does he know about us?"

"Yes."

He blanched and I knew exactly where his thoughts headed. He was afraid of what any guy would be afraid of if he fucked a woman in a relationship. Dan was afraid Brent was going to come down here and cause a scene, possibly cause a physical altercation. Neither Dan nor Brent were built for a tumble and the mental image of the two slapping at each other over me almost made me laugh. I'd never known Brent to be violent until recently when he'd taken to throwing things. Still, he'd missed me when he'd thrown the glass and I assumed that was on purpose. He'd never laid a hand on me the entire time we'd been together.

"Don't worry," I said. "He's not going to do anything."

Dan's shoulders relaxed. "Good." He smiled nervously. "Because not only does he know where I live but he's only a block away. You said he's been acting strange?"

"Yeah. That's not the only reason we split though. There are a lot of other things. Like ten years of things."

"How strange?"

"Very. Like accusing me of poisoning him. Sleepwalking. Eating organ meat. Telling me things I'd seen weren't real."

I neglected to tell him I may have either dreamed some of the stuff or I might be a little out of my head at the moment since I was off my medication.

Gravely, he said, "Has he been drinking the water?"

Not this again. Maybe this was a mistake. I didn't think I could take a spiel about some conspiracy theory but I couldn't help but answer truthfully.

"Yes."

He sighed. "It'll only get worse."

"The way he's acting?"

"Yes. The city will never admit to it and the people are too poor to fight it but they know the water is making people sick and they haven't done a damn thing about it. It screws with some people and makes them paranoid and violent." He rubbed his chest and even though he had a shirt on I knew he was touching one of the scars. "Makes them hallucinate."

I'd written off his prior accusations about the water to him being a conspiracy nut. I thought he might be one of those people who would list off some statistics about how many bacteria and chemicals were in city water as if they'd picked up their information from some bottled water company. It was all bullshit and meant to be used as a scare tactic to get people to buy water. How far were we from purchasing luxury canned air? Artisanal air? Artisanal hose water was exactly what bottled water was. Hell, Ice Mountain was drawn right here in Michigan. So wouldn't that make everyone crazy? I guess reverse osmosis filtered out the crazy. Maybe I needed to be hooked up to a filtration system.

"I know," he said. "You think I'm looney. But I have the scars to prove it." He fingered another scar through his shirt. "Have you drank the tap water?"

I wanted to ask him how he'd gotten the scars but I was reluctant to press the issue. Actually, I was afraid the story he'd tell me might be so fantastical I might question whether moving in with him was a good idea and I figured he'd tell me in his own time.

I finally answered him. "Yes."

"Please don't drink it anymore. I keep plenty of bottled water in the fridge."

I nodded. I wasn't going to argue with him. I would humor him and drink the damn bottled water and hoped it wasn't going to be something he brought up constantly.

He closed the gap between us and wrapped his arms around me and kissed me. The subject was dropped as we consummated my new home.

TWENTY-ONE

MY NERVES WERE put at ease over the next few days. Even though I didn't believe Brent would come to The Mediation Center and cause a scene I kept expecting him to show up and be irate since he'd been acting so weird. But I saw no sign of him other than spotting his car in the driveway of the murder house when I rode with Dan to the store the day after I moved in. I made it a point not to acknowledge the house when we drove by. I didn't know what Brent was up to and I didn't care.

At the store I purchased a small flashlight with a clasp so I could clip it onto my belt loop. Dan had divulged the reason there weren't any lights in the basement and it was going to take me a while to get familiar with the hallway. Apparently, the facility hadn't originally been built with a basement. Since there wasn't much property the church decided the best way to add a few Sunday School classrooms was to take the church donations and put in a basement with a few rooms. The construction company accidentally dug too far and hit an underground tunnel system originally used for utilities that had since been abandoned by the city. By the time the company requested more money to fix the error the funds were depleted. Church attendance plummeted shortly after and within a few years the establishment had gone belly up, leaving a gaping hole at the end of the hallway. Dan found it unsightly and the construction company had failed to install any lighting in the hallway before they'd packed up and left the whole mess for someone else to deal with.

When we'd arrived back from the store and I had a flashlight in hand Dan and I inspected the opening. The end of the hallway was exposed earth and completely unfinished. The floor leading up to it was concrete but you could see where rings of dirt had spread across it, creeping up the hallway. I attributed the musty smell of the hallway to the raw earth.

Dan pointed to the dirt rings on the floor. "When we get heavy rains and the ground gets really saturated it leaks into the basement. Luckily it's never flooded or made it into my place. Just creates a pool of muddy soup on the ground around it, thankfully."

The actual hole was irregular and about four foot in diameter. I shone the light in the hole. The construction company had knocked in the wall of a red brick tunnel. It didn't appear the tunnel had been built for someone to stand fully erect in. An old gas lamp was mounted on the wall about ten feet from the opening.

I said, "There was a hole in the wall of the house's basement. It wasn't open to a tunnel like this though. There was a large pipe but it only looked big enough for someone to crawl through."

"There are a lot of abandoned subways and underground tunnels in cities all over the world. Most of the time the upkeep becomes too expensive and they're deserted."

I shone the light around and inspected the tunnel. "Kinda creepy."

"Really unsightly. Now you know why I never bothered putting any lighting down here."

It was alarming anytime I would descend the stairs once I had the light and it illuminated the opening. It looked ominous and made my skin crawl. I completely understood why Dan had chosen to forgo any lights in the hallway. I was hoping it wouldn't take me long to get used to maneuvering the hallway without a light but I thought knowing the hole was there and not being able to see it might actually be worse. We jokingly dubbed the hole as a gate to hell.

Cohabitation with Dan came naturally. Obviously the first couple of days were filled with fucking way too much, getting high, and not getting a whole lot of anything else done. Our fucking had cured my depression as far as I was concerned. My foggy-headedness lifted. I didn't want to sleep for fourteen hours anymore. And I had a general feeling of contentment I hadn't felt in years.

Everything was going well so I knew—no matter how much I tried to not think about it—that it would all come crashing down sometime or another. I didn't think it would only take a a couple of weeks.

TWENTY-TWO

CONFUSION.

The bed jostled rapidly and Dan cried out. My back was to him and I assumed he was having a bad dream. The sleep was difficult to clear from my brain since we'd gotten high before fucking and turning in for the night. The bed kept bouncing and Dan flailed beside me. He hit me in the back and gripped at my bare skin. We'd both gone to sleep in the nude, as waking up in the middle of the night to have a quickie was pretty common with us. There was a wet smacking sound. Something warm and wet was growing beneath me. Dan's grip loosened.

Smack. Smack. Smack.

"What's going on?" I grumbled as I rolled over.

The faint beam from the night light near the kitchenette was enough to illuminate the scene but my brain struggled to comprehend what I was seeing. Brent was in our place. He was naked and straddling Dan and repeatedly slamming his fists down on his chest. No. He wasn't slamming his fists down on Dan's chest. He had a firm two-handed grasp on the kitchen knife I'd left on the bathroom counter at the house. Brent was stabbing Dan. I screamed and tried to scramble away but ended up falling off the bed.

I tried to get to my feet and slipped several times. I was to my feet before I realized my backside was covered in blood.

Brent continued to stab Dan. Dan lay unmoving. My brain felt like it was on the verge of cutting out. How much trauma could one person take before their brain stopped working?

"Stop!" I shrieked.

I rounded the bed and lunged at Brent. I grabbed at his arms to try to stop him. He jerked away from me and swung both of his fists, still holding the knife, at my face. I saw the knife coming and braced myself for pain, severe disfigurement, possibly death. Instead of stabbing me he managed to backhand punch me in the face. I saw a white-hot flash when my nose broke and I fell to the ground. The pain in my face was tremendous and I could taste blood. Hot blood ran from my nose. I had to keep moving. How long would it be before he turned the knife on me?

Once I had my senses back I realized Brent had stopped stabbing Dan. He lowered his head to Dan's chest and began slurping the blood from one of the wounds.

I got to my feet again and began screaming unintelligibly as I charged him. I had no idea where the knife was and I didn't care. I began beating at Brent's head with my fists but he seemed unfazed. He continued to drink Dan's blood. I tried to grip his arm and pull him off but he was covered in blood and he kept slipping out of my grasp.

I began screaming, "You killed him!" over and over while trying to pull him off Dan.

It quickly became a demented wrestling match on top of Dan. We were both nude and covered in blood and some sick part of my brain thought of those sleazy wrestling matches where the nude or nearly nude girls were covered in baby oil or in a vat of Jell-O. Except our vat was Dan's corpse and his blood was our baby oil.

Brent got away from me and scrambled off the bed. Wherever the knife had been, it clattered to the floor by the bed in the commotion. I jumped for the weapon and my leg got caught up in the blankets and I went headfirst toward the floor. I put my hands out to catch myself and my left wrist popped when my palm hit the floor and pain shot up my forearm. I refused to let the pain stop me and snatched up the knife. The handle was slippery with blood. I gripped it like my life depended on it, which it did, but the firmer my grasp the more the knife wanted to slip out of my hand like a wet bar of soap.

Brent was on his feet and less than five feet from me. He actually hissed at me like a wild animal. I raised the knife and pointed it at him as I slid the rest of the way out of bed. The remnants of the pot were making me clumsy and it was challenging to steady myself. Everything was happening so fast and my vision was swimming.

It was difficult to see in the low lighting but Brent's eyes were wild with something I'd never seen before. Brent wasn't there. He had checked out. And whatever had taken his place was dark and bottomless and inhuman. There was no emotion there.

"You killed him." It was the only thing I could think of to say. I choked back a sob and gagged on the blood running down my throat from my broken nose.

Brent growled and started backing toward the door. I got to my feet, keeping the knife pointed at him. I looked at Dan and could see there was no life left in him and sobbed again.

Brent continued to inch toward the open door. I wasn't sure what to do. Did I try to stop him? Should I wait until he's gone? Was this some elaborate plan of Brent's to frame me for Dan's murder? No. Brent was lost to something I couldn't comprehend.

He dashed out the door.

I ran to the door and shouted, "Stop!"

I couldn't see him but I could hear him scrambling through the hole. I dashed back into the room and found my pants on the floor. My patience and time were gone. I set the knife on the bed and grabbed the flashlight clipped to my belt loop and yanked. The belt loop broke and the flashlight came free. I snatched up the knife with shaky hands and ran out the door, turning on the flashlight as I went.

I approached the hole cautiously, holding the knife and light out. A cold, light breeze came from the hole and made my skin prick and my nipples harden. I shone the light in the hole and looked in to the left and right. To the left, the tunnel continued straight and there was no sign of Brent. To the right, the tunnel made a ninety-degree turn about twenty feet from the hole and the turn was in the direction of the murder house. I listened carefully and thought I could hear the slap of feet but couldn't be sure. I climbed into the hole.

I didn't know why I was following Brent. I should call the cops. But there was some deep pull to avenge Dan's demise. I'd never wanted to hurt anyone, only myself in times of deep depression. I was giving myself over to something I didn't understand and decided to follow it through to the end. If that meant the end of my life or the end of Brent's or both of us, I didn't really care. What did I have left to lose?

The cool breeze that came from the hole was nothing compared to the temperature drop once I was in the tunnel. It felt as though I'd walked into a refrigerator. The flashlight wasn't the greatest and it cast long shadows and did nothing to calm my fears. I tried not to think of the darkness or the unknown or what if I got lost or the tunnel collapsed. I had to catch Brent. Never mind I had no idea what I was going to do with him once I caught up with him. I was going to let instincts take the lead.

The bricks of the tunnel were cold and my feet were starting to go numb. I had to get moving. I dashed down the tunnel but stopped at the turn. For all I knew Brent had stashed another weapon down here and was hiding around the corner, waiting for me to round it so he could kill me. I stood back and shone the light around the corner cautiously. My wrist hurt as I turned it. The pop I'd experienced when I fell on it must've been bad. I held the knife at the ready in my other hand.

Brent wasn't there. Instead I found another long stretch of tunnel. I had no idea how long it went on as the light didn't stretch that far. I could see another tunnel T into the stretch in the distance. I made my way down the path until I reached the T and did another check with the light and knife before proceeding. I tried to gauge how far I would normally walk from The Meditation Temple to the house.

The shadows began to play tricks on me. The fear and adrenaline gave my mind too much fuel and I swore I began to see things in the darkness ahead that my flashlight couldn't reach. I thought I could see the reflection of animalistic eyes with gaping mauls filled with the venomous and dripping fangs of a viper. A hissing sounded somewhere beyond the beam of the flashlight and I knew if there was anything in the darkness it didn't like the light and would stay away as long as my light was working. It dawned on me slowly that I didn't have a light to shine behind me at the same time to keep whatever it was at bay. I found myself spinning in a circle, trying to surround myself with the light. I began to hyperventilate.

Breathe.
Breathe.
Deep breath in.
Deep breath out.
Relax.
Stay Calm.

I took a couple seconds to get reoriented and to make sure I was headed in the right direction. I passed another T in the tunnel before I came to a pipe. It was low and barely big enough to crawl into and as much as I hated the thought of doing so I knew it was most likely the pipe that led to the hole in the basement wall of the house. I involuntarily made a whimpering sound as I dropped to my knees and shone the light in the tunnel. I wasn't sure why I expected Brent to be waiting there to scare the shit out of me but I found the tunnel empty.

I groaned softly as I dropped to my belly. The cold bricks nearly took my breath away. I began to crawl, mindful of the blade of the knife. I could see the light from the basement ahead and stopped. I had a dilemma. There was no way I could make it though the hole quickly. The act of crawling out of the hole would make me vulnerable if Brent was waiting for me. I stilled my breathing and tried to listen. I couldn't hear anything and I had the sudden fear that maybe Brent hadn't come back to the house. Maybe he was still in the tunnel. Maybe he was going to come up behind me. This type of thinking sent me into a panic and I suddenly didn't give a fuck if he was waiting for me in the basement or not. I wanted to get out of the pipe and I wanted out *now*.

In a scramble I managed to nick myself with the knife and bit back a yelp. I ignored the scrapes and future bruises and made my way to the hole as fast as I could. It was definitely the hole for the basement. My fear and panic doubled as I pulled myself through the hole and was greeted by a wordless bellow that nearly made me piss myself.

In the opposite corner of the basement was a man, or what was left of a man, and a chain was padlocked around his neck and attached to an overhead beam. His arm and legs were gone and the remaining stumps were tied off with tourniquets and it appeared the ends had been cauterized, as they were black. He lay in a pool of dried blood and when he opened his mouth to bellow again I noticed his tongue had also been removed.

I covered my mouth, afraid I might vomit. My voice sounded strangled. "Oh my god," I whispered.

The man began to flop around and yell wordlessly.

"Shhh." I held my hands up and realized waving a knife at the guy was probably a bad idea. I could only imagine what I looked like to him. Here was a naked woman emerging from the hole in the wall, covered in blood and dirt and wielding a knife. "I'm not going to hurt you. If you keep making noise he'll know I'm here. Is he upstairs?"

The guy stared at me with glazed eyes and didn't say anything. He waited a beat before he nodded. I made my way toward the stairs and climbed them as soundlessly as I could. The man began to yell again once I was at the top and the sudden break in the silence nearly made me scream out of fright.

The door to the basement was open. All the lights were on but I didn't see any sign of Brent. I could see the kitchen table and the smell hit me as soon as I realized what was on the table. It appeared Brent had wrapped the man's limbs in plastic wrap and left them on the table and the downstairs was swarming with flies. Stacks of paper were strewn about the severed limbs and spilled onto the floor. Maggots covered everything. I spotted a business card for Brent's publisher lying among the wreckage and began to wonder about the identity of the man in the basement.

I cautiously made my way through the living room and went to check the bathroom. The bathroom was empty but there was a stack of yellow legal pads on the counter by the sink and I recognized Brent's nearly illegible scrawl. I picked up one of the notebooks and tried my best to decipher what was written on it but even on the best of days I always had a hard time reading Brent's handwriting. I swear he should've been a doctor.

I dropped the notebooks back on the counter and when I looked up I caught Brent's reflection in the mirror as he stood in the doorway. I spun toward him and lifted the knife and pointed at him.

"Brent, I don't know what's going on but you need help. I think you're sick. I think the water is making you sick. You have to stop drinking the tap water."

He cocked his head like a dog as he stared at me with blank eyes. A fly landed on his forehead but he didn't seem to feel it or couldn't be bothered to swat it away.

"I've been seeing things too."

I'd barely gotten the sentence out when he lunged at me, screaming like a banshee as he did so. As terrified as I was for my life I was also too scared to actually use the knife. And as far gone as Brent was he was still with it enough to know to get the knife away from me. He grabbed my knife-holding wrist with both hands and began to smash my hand against the counter. I still had ahold of the flashlight but my wrist still hurt from the tumble out of the bed. I did my best to try and beat him in the head with the flashlight but only ended up pissing him off. I felt something crack as he slammed my wrist into the counter again and I switched tactics. I raised my knee as hard as I could into his naked crotch.

All the air escaped him and he loosened his grip on my wrist enough that I was able to wrench my hand away. I tried to push him away but he tackled me to the ground. I hit my head on the toilet as I fell and saw stars. He screamed in my face and began clawing at my knife-holding arm above my head. I squeezed the handle of the knife as hot pain shot up my forearm and swung my arm down. The knife landed right below his shoulder blade and his expression changed to one of shock. He began to tremble and opened his mouth. A wet gurgling sound came out before the blood came. I tried to take another breath to scream and I pulled the knife from his back and sunk it into another spot. My wrist screamed in protest. His body jerked with the second knife wound and his body began to go slack. I tried to pull the knife from him but the blood had made it too slippery and my wrist hurt when I tugged at it. I gave him a hard shove and he collapsed beside me on the bathroom floor. He lay on his side, blood spilling from his mouth, as he stared at me in terror and his lips opened and closed like a fish gasping in the open air.

"I'm sorry," I said. "But you killed Dan. And I don't know who the man in the basement is. And you wouldn't snap out of it. If I hadn't done it you would've killed me." I took his hand as he took his last few breaths and once he was gone I cried for a long time.

Later, I woke on the bathroom floor. Flies covered Brent's body. One crawled in and out of his open mouth and a couple others walked over the surface of his open eyes.

I got to my feet and realized I was still holding the flashlight. I dropped it in the sink and stepped out of the bathroom. The floorboards popped as I made my way through the house and tried to avoid any splinters since I didn't have any shoes. The man in the basement screamed. I took a look around the kitchen and didn't see what I was looking for so I took the stairs to our bedroom. There were piles of human excrement in the upstairs hallway, covered in flies, and I gagged several times before entering the bedroom.

I found the cell phone plugged in and fully charged. It was out of minutes but luckily there was still one number that worked no matter what. I dialed the number and listened as it rang twice before someone answered.

"Nine-one-one. Where's the location of your emergency?"

In a calm voice I replied, "Seven thirty-two South Crossley Street."

"What's the nature of your emergency ma'am?"

"There's been a murder."

"A murder? Who am I speaking with?"

"Laura Dyer."

"And who's been murdered?"

"A couple of people. And there's a guy in the basement with no arms or legs."

"Did you say there's a—"

"You need to hurry."

"Ma'am, I need you—"

I hung up the phone and dropped it on the bed. I was halfway down the stairs when the phone started to ring. When I reached the living room I yelled so the man in the basement could hear me, "The police are on their way!"

A wordless bellow responded and I kept going and walked out the front door. The air was cold and raised gooseflesh over my entire body. I stepped out onto the crumbling concrete steps and took a seat next to Dan. He didn't seem to notice the gaping wound in his chest and stomach as he stared up at the sky.

He turned to look at me and said, "The sky is on fire," before he returned his gaze skyward.

I looked to the sky. It was there and it was beautiful and it sang like a siren growing in the distance.

Acknowledgements

A special thanks to Casey Morris for going above and beyond to support artists they enjoy. The world should be filled with art you love and more people like you.

Other **Atlatl Press** Books

No Music and Other Stories by Justin Grimbol
Elaine by Ben Arzate
Fuck Happiness by Kirk Jones
Impossible Driveways by Justin Grimbol
Giraffe Carcass by J. Peter W.
Shining the Light by A.S. Coomer
Failure As a Way of Life by Andersen Prunty
Hold for Release Until the End of the World by C.V. Hunt
Die Empty by Kirk Jones
Mud Season by Justin Grimbol
Death Metal Epic (Book Two: Goat Song Sacrifice) by Dean Swinford
Come Home, We Love You Still by Justin Grimbol
We Did Everything Wrong by C.V. Hunt
Squirm With Me by Andersen Prunty
Hard Bodies by Justin Grimbol
Arafat Mountain by Mike Kleine
Drinking Until Morning by Justin Grimbol
Thanks For Ruining My Life by C.V. Hunt
Death Metal Epic (Book One: The Inverted Katabasis) by Dean Swinford
Fill the Grand Canyon and Live Forever by Andersen Prunty
Mastodon Farm by Mike Kleine
Fuckness by Andersen Prunty
Losing the Light by Brian Cartwright
They Had Goat Heads by D. Harlan Wilson
The Beard by Andersen Prunty

Printed in Great Britain
by Amazon